RUTH

Guillem Viladot (Agramunt, 1922 – Barcelona 1999) was a multi-faceted and prolific writer, artist and contributor to the press whose resistance to authority and questioning of hegemony is written through his entire work. Through novels, fictionalised memoirs, poetry, sculpture, traditional and avantgardist forms, Viladot documents the struggle with lazily accepted paradigms and seeks to carve out a space for the 'self'. This is the story of *Ruth* (2000) too, a short epistolary novel almost without precedent in Spain at the time of its publication and of immense relevance still today, tracing the transition of Raül to Ruth, and in parallel, Ruth's artistic evolution as a young sculptor.

P. Louise Johnson (Matlock, 1970) is Reader in Catalan and Spanish at the University of Sheffield. As an academic she works on modern Catalan and Spanish literature and culture, across gender, sexuality, sport, identity formation and translation. In press is an essay on Josep Pin i Soler's Catalan translation of Thomas More's *Utopia* (1912) (forthcoming in OUP, 2022). Louise's first full-length translation from Catalan, Llorenç Villalonga's *Andrea Víctrix*, was published by Fum d'Estampa in 2021. Her interest in Guillem Viladot stems from a visit to Barcelona in the aftermath of the Sheffield floods of 2007, when she discovered Viladot's short story anthology *Orgànic* in Laie.

'Perniciously relevant... an indispensable novel.'
–Paul Spalding-Mulcock, *Yorkshire Times*

'Viladot is a rebel: insatiable and untiring.'
–Àlex Susanna

'A fundamental figure in the history of Catalan culture [...] difficult
to classify and undisciplined.'
–Pau Minguet

'He never stops experimenting with language. Just when things seem to
be moving along nicely, he looks for other, more provocative, routes.'
–Teresa Ibars

'Ever the apothecary, Viladot mixes poetic and narrative elixirs.'
–Mercè Ibarz

'Guillem Viladot has had the courage to be a pioneer in a country where any attempt at creation is criticised from an obtuse and deep-seated
position of conservatism.'
–Ignasi Riera

'No matter the expressive medium: be it discursive, visual, object or
concrete poetry [...] the conduit [...] is always Viladot himself. That is,
his dissident and marginal *self* facing up to different forms of power.'
–J. Pont

This translation has been published in Great Britain
by Fum d'Estampa Press Limited 2022
001

Original Catalan title: *Ruth*, first published in 2000
All rights reserved

The moral rights of the author and translator have been asserted
Set in Adobe Garamond Pro

Printed and bound by Great Britain by CMP UK Ltd.
A CIP catalogue record for this book is available from the British Library

ISBN: 978-1-913744-06-9

The publication has been made possible thanks to the Fundació Viladot – Lo Pardal, Càtedra Màrius Torres – Universitat de Lleida, and the Ajuntament d'Agramunt.

CENTENARI
GUILLEM VILADOT
1922-2022

FUM D'ESTAMPA PRESS

RUTH

GUILLEM VILADOT

Translated by

P. LOUISE JOHNSON

RUTH

PRELUDE

I often attend exhibitions at the Espai Guinovart. They're always interesting, although of course the quality can be variable and some artists are more original than others.

That Sunday I was looking forward with relish to the Joan Hernández Pijuan opening. The master's works exude a lyrical, earthy, very human quality, but we need to keep in mind his words of caution: *'These papers and canvases may appear finished in the workshop, but until they emerge into public view, there'll always be a risk that I change something, because their very presence makes me doubt myself, and new ideas begin to prick at me. When they're exhibited, they take on this 'other' reality as their context changes, and they leave behind the studio where they've been created and in some way conditioned. They cease being objects for my personal use, and in the neutral exhibition space, open to other gazes, they assume their own reality. They become objects for communal reflection. Exhibition is the culmination of their purpose.'*

There was a notable presence of writers and artistic folk who had come to celebrate with our friend Joan Hernández Pijuan at the Espai Guinovart; pretty much all of us were there. After the formal opening ceremony, we were served the now traditional aperitif of cava and flatbreads.

Amid the melee of guests, I caught sight of a couple about my age accompanied by a young woman who couldn't have been more than twenty. As they made their way towards me, I realised it was Ivars the painter, and his wife. We hadn't met for years and greeted each other warmly.

'Do you know our daughter?' he asked pointedly.

'I'm not sure I've had the pleasure.'

'When you met her, she was our son…'

'I'm sorry?'

'She used to be Raül, or still is, but she wants to be Ruth, which is why she's dressed as a female. We're in a process of transition.'

I must have looked utterly confused because my friend Ivars straightaway clarified, 'She wants to change sex and name.'

Ivars' wife started crying as I had to stop myself blurting out, 'What, just like that?'

'It's been really difficult, you know, we're struggling to cope.'

Meanwhile, Ruth, formerly Raül, was smiling at me. Her father seemed nervous. Once I'd recovered my composure, I observed the girl in front of me carefully. She was extremely pretty, bright eyes, a perfect oval face, shapely lips and long mahogany-tinted hair. She was slim, and her fingers were long and delicate. What most aroused my curiosity was her skin, and her face in particular. I was so taken by it that in a move most unlike me, I asked her:

'Do you mind?' And without waiting for an answer, I stroked her cheek with my right hand.

'Incredible.'

My friend Ivars managed a smile, while his wife still whimpered. With an easy familiarity, Ruth asked me to show her around the Espai Guinovart. This is something I love doing, and I always begin with an anecdote to set my audience at ease.

'Well, Ruth, a long time ago this was a Mercedarian convent. The space now dedicated to Josep Guinovart's work would have been the cloister. The lower floor was occupied by a range of municipal offices, and the first floor hosted the local primary school. When I was a child I came here every day for lessons. As you can imagine, this place is close to my heart. I was happy here because I had a great teacher, mestre Agustí Faixa, who was a devil for insisting we read, and had us make chessboards and chess pieces out of cane. The convent was demolished in 1936, and in 1948 the General Directorate for Devastated Regions built a market here, and the Espai Guinovart is now housed within that structure.'

As we made our way around, Ruth and I didn't stop talking. I'm not sure she was always attentive, but I owed her the full tour.

'Every piece exhibited here speaks to the strength of the artist's roots in this landscape. Although he wasn't born locally, his mother was from Agramunt. Guino lived here around 1938, and after the war he used to come back every summer to live the life of a peasant, in a hut, with a small holding.

'You love this land too, don't you?'

'Perhaps that's why Guino's work means so much to me.'

I explained to Ruth that the space is divided into three main sectors or elements: Seasons, Hut, and Threshing Floor. Around them, the myth is completed by wheat, straw, fire, and a firmament of stars, the aesthetic dimension that transcends reality. We made our way to the Threshing Floor.

'Look, how marvellous! The threshing floor sublimely interpreted as the miraculous centre of peasant life and tradition: the domestic, social and economic nucleus. The peasant is the incarnation of the land-become-symbol, the stubbornness of a constant, dark struggle against adverse forces of nature. The artist has given shape to the almost mystical value of the peasant by elevating it above simple anecdote.'

Ruth came close and looked at me with delighted surprise.

'I want to be able to love as you love: to love people, the land, reality, dreams... my body, and others' bodies. Who am I, my friend? What sense of oneness do you have, all of you who have so much love? Where does your satisfaction with life come from? My friend, you haven't had to make a choice, you've just lived the life that you've been given, like a destiny that someone has picked out for you and guides you. I, on the other hand, have to choose.'

There's nothing I could do to stop my eyes from tearing up, but I pretended not to notice.

'Thanks to Guinovart, this rebellious landscape has been projected worldwide as an embassy of everything else that our country is: the humble heroism of warm colours and uninhabited immenseness, converted by the genius of the artist into cradle and language of solidarity, fraternal embers of hope.'

Ruth grabbed my hand and squeezed it hard. And as though mimicking the age-old rhythm of the field roller, we walked again and again around the edge of the Threshing Floor. As she gazed up,

Ruth implored: 'I want to rise up above this starry constellation, and unleash a cascade of love on you all.' Falling silent, she then said: 'What love, though, if I still don't love myself…?' She gave me a hug and whispered into my ear: 'I hate my mother…'

The Ivars family said goodbye. Ruth followed, saying: 'I'll write to you.'

Letter 1

Dear friend,

I arrived home yesterday (I live alone). I accompanied my parents to the Espai Guinovart because they wanted to see you again and introduce me to you. I don't spend much time with them. I'm sure mother wishes she could harangue me more often. Father tends to keep a prudent distance and respects my freedom. I get on very badly with mother. Her first child was a daughter, so she was desperate for a son. When the midwife announced after a difficult birth that she had a son, she burst into floods of tears, tears of gratitude. She's told me all about it many times to the point that now, given my status, it comes across as a reproach. She has never forgiven me for the fact that the birth of that child was a negative event, or subversive, and that her son, Raül, now wishes to be her daughter, Ruth. Because mothers carry and give birth to their children, they seem to think they have the right to treat them as their property, particularly the males. Giving birth to a daughter was a symmetry, and as symmetry the daughter became a calque of the mother herself and of little interest, whereas giving birth to a son, a male, was an act that complemented her essence as a woman in the sense of supplementing the absence or lack that she seemed to experience as a female, as though engendering a male might equate to conquering the penis she has never had. Mother has internalised this fantasy so completely that she has never forgiven me for being born male, or for having always felt myself to be female and wanting to become a woman, because that is what I most desire and because that is how I can realise to the fullest degree the female condition that has been a part of me since my earliest infancy. That's when I remember first hanging around with the girls, and especially going to the toilet alongside them, peeing with them. When the schoolmistress found

13

out, she told my mother straight away, as if I'd committed some awful impertinence. From that day forwards, mother dressed me in unequivocally masculine clothing in the hope that the girls themselves would recognise me as an imposter and exclude me from their groups. But her plan misfired because the girls felt comfortable around a little sissy boy like me. When the grown-ups realised that clothes alone weren't enough, I was transferred to a boys' school.

The pre-school director was horrified when she discovered that I peed like a woman, squatting down, not standing up like a man. When this came to mother's attention she had such a fit of hysterics they had to call the doctor. And after that upset, mother had me undergo clinical tests to find out once and for all what was going on. As I sat naked on the examination couch, the doctor scrutinised me front and behind, and with gravitas, concluded that I was a boy, male. And he added, with some hesitation in his voice, that perhaps my willy was a tad underdeveloped, but my anatomy was certainly sufficient to certify my maleness. He also added that in time it would grow to normal size... When mother recounted these things to me, it was to validate one version of my history over another.

My friend, can you imagine how many times I've had to get undressed to have my genitalia examined? If I don't bore you too much, I'll tell you all about them. This is my first letter, and I don't want to write pages and pages. But I thought that because you're a writer, and you explore the human condition, you might be interested in the experience I'm living through. Please don't feel that you have to respond, I know you're busy; it's enough that you read what I write.

Thank you for your company at the Espai Guinovart. Please let me know next time you exhibit there. I know that you showed a series of object poems there under the title *Self*, themed around key psychoanalytic concepts. Since you have an interest in this Freudian discipline, I'm sure you'll be curious to hear about my transsexuality. I'm familiar with your novels and I've always been fascinated by the psychological analysis of characters. Perhaps, as in my case, you will never fully know how an individual's conduct can lead to such major modifications of their condition; we're not talking about anomalies of behaviour or psychic illnesses, but about the will, the desire, to be what we feel ourselves to be. A psychiatric professional labelled me neurotic and psychotic, not realising that I'm prepared to leave behind everything I'm not, and if that creates conflicts it's because of the antinomy between a real sexual instinct that doesn't correspond to my current genitalia and the socialisation that configures the individual as a person of the opposite sex, focussed solely on the genitals. This is my war: my genitals, genitals as the universal referent above any other consideration that organizes humanity into groups of males and groups of females. Anyone who doesn't fit easily into those categories is ill. No! Nature isn't always so well-ordered and it often creates individuals who defy classification: feeling oneself to be a woman, possessing male genitalia. Which is my case. What do I need a penis for if I feel like a woman?

I hope you'll accept me for who I really am.

Be well.
Ruth

Letter 2

My friend,

The first letter I wrote finishes with a reference to the will to stop being what I'm not. But what do I want to be? On the one hand there's the conflict between the concrete anatomy that shapes me and the sylph that generates the substance of my spirit. On the other, I'm faced with the added conflict of everyday socialisation via environmental pressure which seeks to determine what my personality should be, regardless of who I am as an individual, and based only on collective identifiers. We have to conclude that a person is born to become an integral part of society and to obey its directives.

While I was still a very young child I became aware of this turmoil by experiencing it. I had male (though underdeveloped) genitals, but I felt like a girl, and this feeling clashed with the firm conviction of my mother, who insisted I was male. I peed like a girl and I dressed like a girl. In secret, of course. I tried on my sister's dresses and gazed at myself in the mirror; I looked good and felt comfortable. The mirror reflection that always told me the truth. I was here and on the other side, in the mirror, I was the same. Sometimes, if I looked really good, I had the urge to go through the mirror to the other side, to a reality disconnected from the conventionalisms that surrounded me. The only thing that jarred slightly was my hairstyle, and over time I allowed my hair to grow longer, despite my mother's rebukes. In the end she had to give in because boys started wearing their hair longer, imitating photos published in the gossip magazines. My sister was enthusiastic about my outfits and encouraged me to continue. She saw it as a game and didn't understand that I needed to dress this way to materialise what I felt, to configure my internal disposition externally, to visually proclaim the desire that drove me to reject my physical circumstance, and embrace its contrary.

As time went by and I reached adolescence, wearing underwear gave me the most pleasure. My sister was almost two years older than me and handed down whatever she had grown out of. I viewed those delicate garments as proof of my womanhood. Putting on panties became almost liturgical, a sacrament. You could have said that my pubis was transformed into a tender, delicate cadence, my penis disappearing as though it had never existed. And I would rush to the mirror for credible witness of my changed state. My torso was still smooth and bore no signs of breasts beginning to grow. Even so, this didn't put me off wearing a bra. As I gazed at myself in the mirror I had no doubt that one day I would have woman's breasts, perhaps small because of my figure, but attractive nonetheless. It was just a matter of time. A teenage girl has her whole life and every triumph ahead of her.

One Sunday I took advantage of being in the house alone to dress up in my sister's dresses and lingerie. I modelled them gracefully and glided elegantly around the room imagining myself to be a lady of great beauty with a long train of admirers. Men who gradually came into focus in the mirror, consorts of my body who exalted my beauty. Men who loved me. This mirroring caused such intense arousal that I was overcome by convulsions deep inside that shook me to the core. Spasms that blacked out everything external to me.

'Your first orgasm,' my sister said. I didn't know what she was talking about. She educated me as I explained what had happened. 'Did your penis get hard?' 'No.' 'Did it get bigger?' 'No.' 'And the whole of your body spasmed?' 'Yes.' 'Describe it.'

'It began as a really pleasant arousal that gradually intensified until spasms exploded in waves and then receded before growing to a climax again. Like that, four or five times.'

My sister took my penis in her hand and asked: 'Did anything come out?'

'No, nothing.'

Then she looked me in the eyes and, like a judge passing sentence, said: 'You had a female orgasm.'

I thought she was about to start crying but I couldn't have been more wrong. Still looking at me, she said: 'What's going on with you, Raül?' And she burst out laughing.

That was a time when she had lots of boyfriends and knew very well what both female and male orgasms were like. She was very open with me.

'The male orgasm is a single ejaculation. The climax is short, the spasms less powerful and the resolution is quick.' And as though she were an expert, she added: 'The female orgasm involves the whole body; the male just the penis…'

When she'd finished the masterclass, I started laughing too and shouted hysterically:

'I'm a woman! I'm a woman…!'

I twirled around the room in frilly knickers and bras, leaping theatrically onto the bed and making such a racket that mother appeared. She stood stock-still at the sight of me. When she'd gathered herself, she asked us what was going on. I was drunk on euphoria and mother's presence wasn't going to dampen my celebrations. I shouted out unbridled:

'I'm a woman! I'm a woman!'

'Be quiet!' mother ordered.

I ignored her, instead repeating compulsively: 'I'm a woman, I'm a woman, I'm a woman!'

And with new-found courage I added 'And now you have two daughters! Yes, yes, yesss!'

From then on I dressed as a woman twenty-four hours a day. In the Fine Arts Faculty no-one batted an eyelid, or maybe just a bit, because almost all the girls wore jeans, and I rocked up in short skirts. Mother's reaction was dramatic: 'If you want to dress like a slut you can get out and stay out.' Father was more sardonic: 'Transvestites can have a great life if they choose the right street corner…'

Once the commotion had died down, I begged mother to listen to me, to put her demons to one side. 'Things are how they are, and you're not going to change them…'

'You're coming to the doctor with me.'

There was no sense in creating more fuss so I agreed. I wasn't risking anything because my proof of identity, my female orgasm, confirmed that I was a woman. And so whatever the doctor or doctors might say – and there have been a lot –, not one of them, nor any of their diagnoses, theories or therapies, could erase what I'd experienced: the definitive testimony of my female nature.

Before the doctor's appointment, I talked to my sister about the possibility of my having, let's say, an intimate encounter with one of her friends, and she said she'd arrange it. It was at one of their houses. The lad was clear from the start that he was comfortable with a young woman of my… characteristics. We started kissing and caressing each other.

'Take your clothes off,' he said, as he undressed. I saw he had a full erection. When he saw me completely naked, his erection softened. He was very open with me, saying that although my sister had explained the situation clearly, words were one thing and reality quite another. And as though wanting to justify himself, he went on, 'Even though your sister put me in the picture, your face, the way you move, dress, everything about you… it was a real surprise seeing your penis.' Sitting on the bed, he studied me: 'From the back you're a very good-looking girl.'

He made me lie next to him, face down, and began to massage and kiss my butt cheeks. When he slipped a finger into my anus I span round. His erection had returned. Now it was me kissing him. His penis stiffened. From his lips I kissed his chest, his abdomen and then genitals, perhaps a little mechanically, but willingly, with real desire, just as my sister had instructed me. The game aroused me, and him. Our embrace was so fierce that ecstasy came quick. Just before that, he tried to penetrate me anally, but he was too late, and I wouldn't have let him anyway. He collapsed into a generous orgasm, and I joined him.

Again, I had my confirmation: I was a woman. That was a properly scientific experiment in arousal, to gain knowledge, learn about effects and draw conclusions. I was a woman. It had happened just the same as the first time. A calque. And just as I celebrated this victory, I realised that in order to be completely a woman, outside as well as within, I had a long road ahead of me.

My friend: I think the most fundamental part of me was in place then. But there were aspects of my conflict that I needed to resolve, external aspects such as family and social pressure that weren't and aren't allowing me to rid myself of all obstacles to freedom. With my profound conviction and stubbornness, I'll get there.

Be happy.
Ruth

My friend,

Was the evidence of female orgasms enough to feel female? I thought, and experienced, like a woman. Was that sufficient? Perhaps my arousal was artificially induced? Or maybe my body needed to be penetrated fully before I could really know myself? I had no desire whatsoever to have homosexual experiences, so I needed to think how I could fulfil my true nature. As this went on, I realised I was too self-contained, too focussed on myself. I was isolated from my surroundings. What I mean, my friend, is that in order to be a complete woman, I needed one thing to happen: really know what it is to love, to love a man with the sensibility of a woman.

And this happened one summer at the beach. I'd gone there with my sister and some of her friends. We messed around, played volleyball, sunbathed. As I lay in the sun wearing only a tanga, a young man stopped and said: 'What a beautiful body!' He was gazing admiringly at me. He sat down by my side and smiled. Suddenly, and to my surprise, he asked, 'What did you do with your breasts?'

I smiled, half-startled, half-grateful. He apologised clumsily, but with kindness, and my imagination lit up: congeniality was the answer. I would sew together the best parts of me with the thread of congeniality and win him over, but without sacrificing the determination not to be what I'm not. We chatted for a while, and then he revealed that he'd just finished a degree in Communications Engineering.

'And what do you do?'

'Fine Arts. I'm Ruth, by the way. What's your name?'

'Raül.'

'No!' I shouted.

'No what?'

'Nothing, it doesn't matter.'

For a few seconds we looked at each other and it was as though the penny had dropped for both of us.

'Let's go for a drink,' he said.

The club was packed and we danced only briefly. It was just too busy and impossible to move. The bar was several people deep and no-one was moving.

'Shall we go outside?'

The big terrace was almost deserted. We sat on the grass in a corner.

'You're very pretty. I like you, I'm attracted to you... Ruth.'

'I like you too, Raül...'

My voice shook as I said his name. He kissed me softly, respectfully. Sitting there on the grass, we squeezed each other's hands tight and I felt a pulse of excitement. That instant seemed timeless. As if on autopilot, we went back into the club to say goodbye to my friends, but there was no sight of them. His car was outside. Before we got moving, he kissed me again. About half a mile from the club the traffic cops pulled us over. They breathalysed Raül because he was driving, but when they realised there wasn't a trace of alcohol in his system, they asked us both for our papers, presumably to justify the stop.

'You're name's Raül. And you're Raül too?'

'I'm Ruth.'

'Your licence says Raül.'

'It does at the moment...'

That was all they got out of us before they went back to their car. My friend took my licence and read my name.

'They're right, it says Raül.'

'And...?'

'What do you mean, and?'

I wasn't in the mood for explanations. We drove back to my sister's house where I'd been staying since the row with my parents and I invited him in. The house was empty and I poured him a glass of wine.

'Have a seat. I'll answer your question now.'

I undressed in front of him. When he saw me naked he blinked hard, too surprised to speak. After a minute or two he found his tongue.

'Your body is enchanting. I want you…'

He was beginning to get aroused. He came up and kissed me, kissed all of my body, or that's how it felt. He was tactful enough not to mention my penis, and so I did.

'You want my body, Raül, but it's not complete. Rather, it's not enough.'

Immediately he got my drift and replied, 'Genitals aren't everything, Ruth. They're certainly important, but other things – eyes, voice, skin, feelings, intellect – are just as interesting, if not more so.' He was silent a few moments and then continued: 'You can make love with all of those things.'

'But what kind of love?'

'Love that transcends the body, desire. Love is esteem, admiration…'

'Yes, Raül, I know, but I want it all, flesh and spirit, because we are this totality, we have to be this totality, this sum of everything. When you love me I want to feel you penetrating me…'

Excited by my own words, I asked Raül to take off his clothes.

'You'll see the difference. You're a whole man and I'm a malformed woman.'

'No, you're not! You're a girl who just needs retouching slightly.'

He accepted me as I was, as a love object he hadn't chosen but whom he welcomed as our two lives converged. As we lay on the bed next to each other, I was happy. Perhaps not so much at the immediate situation as at the excitement and expectation of the process that lay before me, which could be completed successfully. I took his penis gently into my hand.

'You're very well-endowed…'

I kissed him. He embraced my whole body. It occurred to me then that a woman's sex is all our body, that the whole body is sex, sexuality, desire. I felt his erection between my thighs.

'Hold me tighter…'

I was aroused. Our kisses, lips, hands, were ferocious, our skin tingled with the vibrations of a single, indivisible psyche. His sex was hard. I moistened it with saliva so as to encompass it all.

'One day it will be inside me... and we'll be one flesh.'

'We already are,' he said, barely able to get the words out. At that moment unstoppable waves of electricity pulsed through my entire body, as if every light in the city had suddenly been switched on.

Taking this as permission, he came in my mouth in spurts of honeyed salt. This scene was as far removed from my two or three earlier sexual experiences as it is possible to imagine. This encounter with Raül had been a confirmation on multiple levels of my nature. I had fallen in love with Raül. The man who shared my name seemed purged of masculinity as he became the purifier of my narrative. This was the beginning of my future.

Be well.
Ruth

Letter 4

My dear friend,

I registered a request to be exempted from military service, and I've received an official notification letter instructing me to attend a medical review. First, I should tell you that between my last letter and this, I've done a lot of thinking and have been very anxious. I can't stop wondering whether I'm deluding myself about my encounters with men. I'm not questioning the facts, obviously, because sex is sex, but I'm doubting the conclusions I draw from sex, suspecting that I may have invented them to suit my purposes. Nervous exaggerations, fantasies that shape my desire according to preconceived ideas aligned with well-established social commonplaces. Are the same thoughts being undermined in the same way as always? And on top of that, the letter from the military.

I'm scared. The army is a macho collective in which I have no confidence whatsoever. They will look at me, examine me, they'll subject me to all manner of indecencies to satisfy the sick curiosity of their power-hungry instincts.

In order to arm myself ahead of what might happen with the military, I've arranged an appointment with a psychoanalyst who's been recommended to me. I could have chosen a female psychologist, but I prefer the professional to be male, perhaps because I imagine he'll have direct experience of male-male confrontation.

No sooner do I arrive at his practice than I break down in tears as if my defences have abandoned me. He's a middle-aged man who inspires confidence. For minutes neither of us speaks, and then when he asks me if I'd like something to drink, I make a fragmented, faltering attempt at communication.

'No, thank you… I confess I chose to see you because I don't know who I am. Please don't refer me to some community or family help group.' Once I'd found my voice, it was easy. 'From the waist up I'm a girl, adolescent maybe, and from the waist down I'm a boy who hasn't matured since infancy.'

When I put it like that, I feel like a minotaur or something, but instead of half man and half bull, I'm a girl and boy in equal parts. No: ninety percent woman, and the rest, infant male. I tell him my story, and he listens attentively before asking me a series of very specific questions, and then beckoning me to undress.

'Smooth skin,' he says, 'and not a hair of a beard or anywhere on your body...' He examines my penis. 'You are only the second case of intersexuality I've come across.' His tone is familiar, even cordial. He acknowledges, as I already know, that the two adversaries most dangerous to my reality are my family, especially mother, and society. 'Society, because its identity paradigms are excessively masculine and will only make life difficult for you.'

I get dressed and he adds:

'But forced feminisation could also be dangerous for you. Don't go down the road of risky sexual encounters because they could end up making you believe things that are no more than fantasies.'

I admit that I'm in love with a boy.

'That's fine, provided you can distinguish between sexual relations that are emotionally motivated, and what we might call gratuitous hook-ups.'

He then has me sit down in front of him and looks at me with almost scary gravitas, concluding,

'If you want to be a woman, you'll need to undergo a course of hormone therapy and see how that works out, before we think about surgery. One thing is certain: you can't go on like this.'

I'm quite cheerful when I come out of his office and tell my sister what he's said when I get home. 'I'll help you,' she promises, before convincing me that we need to explain the situation to our family, because we'll need money.

'I really can't face another row with mother, hear her say that she should have aborted me, that she's given birth to a monster. I can't bear her egotistical posturing, so proud to be the mother, owner even, of a male.'

My sister reassures me and says she'll sort everything, and I wait for a few days before we visit. As soon as she opens the door, she goes for the jugular: 'Oh look, it's the family poofter.' Dad is there, a few of my aunts and uncles too; almost the whole family, in fact. Mother looks round to check people's reactions, and adds, 'Just so you know, if you're a homosexual, there's a cure now, and if you want to be cured, we'd be happy to pay for the treatment.'

I bite my tongue, but only until she launches a scathing attack on the way I'm dressed, comparing me to a Parisian whore. I wasn't taking any more.

'You've got the wrong end of the stick, mother. I'm not ill, I was just born wrong. I'm your daughter.'

'Oh, Raül's a lady now! You're sick. You're a sick poofter.'

I explode.

'It's not my fault I was born wrong, nothing to do with me what happened in your womb, this twisted geniture; it's not down to me that you're too stubborn to see that I was half aborted, that your blind obsession with having a son has demented you and turned you into my most egregious enemy...' At that moment I am overcome by hatred, and my screaming and crying crystallizes in a single word:

'Bitch!!'

My sister grabs hold of me and leads me away into a room next door. I can hear mother, still shouting:

'Bitch or not I swear that you'll be a man, because that's what I want. You can hide yourself in dresses, but you're a man. Understand?!'

I sob bitterly but my sister keeps a cool head: 'She's offered to pay, so let's take the money and then see.'

We come back into the sitting room and I go up to my mother, apologise, and agree to do what she thinks best. 'But on condition that I undergo therapy alone, without anyone else there.'

She looks at me, unsure at first.

'Keep me informed, and come by whenever you want, but dressed as a man.'

My father is as pragmatic as my sister, and says: 'Open an account wherever you want, and send me the details.'

27

Finally back outside, my legs turn to jelly and my sister has to take my whole weight on her arm and shoulder.

'Let's go and have dinner.'

We walk a while first, until my head is clear of the family hostility. And then suddenly we're overcome with a sense of euphoria, as though we've won an unexpected victory. We run, laugh, and people look at us, but we don't care. Without warning, my sister suggests: 'Perhaps you'd be better off living on your own.'

Be happy.
Ruth

Letter 5

My dear friend,

I've done my duty by the military! I turn up to my appointment at the army offices, admittedly more dolled-up than usual: I'm wearing a very tight leather miniskirt, an orange blouse, black stockings and stilettos, and just some eyeshadow by way of make-up. As I approach the gateway to the main building, a guard blocks my path. Suddenly I'm confronted by more soldiers wearing armbands marked 'MP'.

'This isn't a knocking shop, sweets.'

'How much for a blowie?'

'Hold your horses, love.'

My hatred for these idiots knows no limits, but I keep my composure and hand over my papers. The guard calls the corporal, and the corporal goes off to find the sergeant.

'What's going on, lads?'

The sergeant looks at the papers and then looks at me, perplexed, before signalling wearily that I should accompany him. We walk along corridor after corridor, and every time we come across soldiers, they greet me with 'I'd give her one' or similar. Finally we stop and the sergeant knocks at a door.

'Come.'

'Sir, it's the lad who's here for the appointment: Raül Ivars Comelles.'

The captain who receives us is a strapping, good looking youth. He glances at me, unperturbed.

'Take a seat.'

I sit down daintily, like a schoolgirl.

'Why are you dressed like that?'

He doesn't let me answer.

'You're Raül Ivars Comelles, Fine Arts student, correct? How do you fund yourself?'

'I have a grant, and a monthly allowance from my father.'

'How long have you cross-dressed? Do you take drugs? Are you being exploited? Do you have a pimp? Are you homosexual?'

The questions don't stop. I start crying. All the while, the captain is typing. He takes the sheet out of the typewriter and hands it to me.

'Take this to room 7-B. They're expecting you.'

An orderly leads the way. He knocks at a huge door. Again, a voice: 'Come.' Two majors and a colonel are sat at the table. They invite me to sit down across from them.

'Over to you, the floor's yours. Speak freely.'

I hand them the captain's report but the colonel doesn't even look at it.

'Please, go ahead. Speak.'

I take a deep breath and start: 'First of all I'd like to clarify that I'm not homosexual. I have what might be referred to as a birth defect which isn't anatomically dominant, and my psyche is female. Apparently I'm what's known as an intersexual or transsexual.

'And how do you know all that?'

'I'm seeing a psychoanalyst and endocrinologist.'

'Stand up and take your clothes off. All of them.'

Once I'm naked he examines me close up, looking for male body hair. He prods my chest, my abdomen, and shoulders, and has me perform a series of contortions. Then with two fingers he taps my penis. Finally he turns to his colleagues: 'If there's anything else...'

One of the majors indicates he wants to examine my anus. They ask me to bend over and touch my toes. A soldier gloves up and, separating my buttocks, explores my anus. I'm not concerned; I'd never been sodomised. In the meantime, the colonel is writing up his own report. It ends with three words: 'normal anal state'.

'Take this to office 12 and introduce yourself to the captain.'

The captain is older and has a kind face. Straightaway he offers me a seat and asks me to explain my situation. 'I want to know about your life.'

Halfway through my account a sergeant enters with a pile of papers from which the captain selects a sheet, the certificate that will either save me or condemn me to the world of compulsive males. He is well aware of my anticipation. He signs it, and hands it to me saying, 'Whether you're a boy or a girl, you'd do well to dress differently. This isn't you. Be more discreet. Don't exaggerate that which you still aren't...' And he adds: 'I'll see you out.' We shake hands firmly. 'Good luck; you'll need it...'

I think every single sentry is watching. I walk a few steps and then stop to read the piece of paper: 'I, the undersigned, President of the Military Medical Commission, certify that Raül Ivars Comelles is exempted from military service...'

I burst out laughing in spite of myself. This is my victory against a whole establishment of males. How many people just like me, desperate and abandoned, have had to turn to prostitution and ended up slaves in a callous empire of men! I can still feel the pressure of the captain's handshake, and I kiss its imprint on my hand. Then I throw up over the roots of a nearby tree.

I don't want to be part of some privileged group either by default or through merit. My singularity isn't some kind of special qualification. I just want to be a normal woman... What is a normal woman? From now on I'm going to do everything possible to make it happen. I'll finish my Fine Arts degree and work, work to become a woman, a normal woman, but different in my own way. Because surely all women are different and no two are exactly alike? I don't want to be like my sister or mother. I want to be the woman that fits my idea of a woman: a nice body, intelligent, and capable of falling in love with a man... And I want to live on my own.

I'm talking aloud to myself.

Perhaps you're wondering what's happened to Raül. I haven't heard from him in days. I know I have to let him know how things are going. Am I still in love with him? Or do I just not want to feel as though I'm completely alone? I enjoy being on my own but, at the same time, sometimes solitude isn't good for me. Every time I think of him a shiver goes through me. Is he really interested in me as I am, though, or does he see me as something of a charity case, in need of protection? Away from my family and safe now from the military, I feel more like myself than ever. But 'I' am still to be defined, the I that exists inside and shapes my actions. Perhaps I've asked you before: why are people divided into men and woman by sex, rather than by other characteristics which might be just as, if not more, important? Might sex be a trap that humanity has fallen into since the beginning of everything? Why hasn't culture overcome this servitude? Why should culture, with the complicity of society, still be shackled by nature? But perhaps not all society is so complaisant. I'm just musing. I keep thinking about all of those others who, for whatever reason, have had to deny their sexuality, and exist on the margins as though it were the most normal, most legitimate thing in the world.

Now that I feel freer than I ever did, I'm beginning to suspect that there's more to it than sexuality, and that desire can be sublimated in other directions, just as the psychoanalyst suggested. Maybe it can, but my sex is at the root of this whole confusion. This isn't satisfaction rhetoric, and I'm not trying to justify myself or hoist my singularity as some kind of unique identifier. Let me think. What happens if once I've had surgery I still can't be the woman I want to be? I know I will be, though: a wrong body put right, and the desire to improve further.

Social convention determines that people should marry, have children, and earn money. Is that all there is? The way things work seems to be determined by the majority's acceptance of what are believed to be the most propitious behavioural norms. And what if instead of nature and society, I am pure spirit: thought, feeling, will…? Without the army on my back, I feel such relief, free of the burden of machismo, as if I've left my penis behind in the process, a mockery of a penis but a terrible burden nonetheless. I'm a woman: my body is pure, my thoughts immaculate… I am myself, liberated from every mark of servitude. I am an angel, like one of those you discovered in the desert that summer. My friend, do I come across as nonsensical because I think and formulate ideas that the huge majority of people are incapable of taking on board? If my body is without equal, can't my thoughts be too? And be able to shout about it! Or are minorities, the marginalised, those who are rare or different… condemned to remain silent, voiceless, unable to make their singular condition heard, no matter how worthy of merit? It's all so complex, I know. Has it always been like this?

Be well.
Ruth

Letter 6

Dear friend,

At the beginning of this correspondence I told you that I felt as though I was a woman. Don't be surprised by my saying so again; we'll keep coming back to it. I also confessed to you that I understood love as an urge whose objective was the penetration of a woman by a man. But now, suddenly, I'm repulsed: why should I have to accept such a sexist model? Why should I want them to make me a vagina simply for the satisfaction of men? Surely my love for Raül and the orgasms we shared skin on skin without any possibility of penetration, surely these weren't just imagined, unreal presences of how normal women behave, phantom acts that I can never achieve in my estranged natural state? But that doesn't erase my need to love, and to be loved: that's a sentiment that comes from deep inside, so thoroughly written through me that I cannot ignore its urging. Sometimes when my letters to you become more rhetorical, I think perhaps that I should give up on sculpture and start writing instead, to purge myself of this whole mess. Who knows, one day I might do just that.

I'm still being treated by the psychoanalyst and the endocrinologist, who has told me that if my breasts don't increase in volume, he'll give me silicone implants. I'm really not keen on the idea, because it means making my body more artificial. The psychoanalyst meanwhile never tires of saying that he has no intention of dictating behavioural paradigms for me to follow like an automaton. He encourages me to make up my own mind on the basis of how other women behave. One day when I insist to him that I feel like a woman, he asks:

'What kind of woman?'

'Female. Because I've had a woman's orgasms.'

'And how do you know they were orgasms, and female?'

'Because my sister explained them to me, and they didn't just happen once.'

'Hasn't it occurred to you that your sister might simply have extrapolated from her own experience? Whatever the reality, it is an individual's reality, and you have your own. Whatever anyone else says about your reality is merely an interpretation. Your own experience is not transferable, and it can never simply be the calque of someone else's. And vice-versa: another person's experience and yours are not symmetrical. You are you, in relation to yourself, and not in function of other people's reality.'

My friend, that was hard to take! I thought I had all the evidence I needed with my hairless body and spasms of pleasure. Now it turns out that almost everything is open to question. Perhaps I'm neither a man, nor a woman, nor anything concrete. Perhaps my life is just ambiguity, uncontrolled, without horizons, or even ports where I might tie up and steady myself. I am not identifiable outside of myself. In other words, I need to anchor myself within me, as well as in the examination of someone who is not me.

I shout out, 'I want someone to love me, I want love, I'm begging for someone to let me love them…'

There's a deathly silence before the psychoanalyst says, 'Begin by loving yourself, and this love will be complete when – if – you accept yourself fully.'

He's clever! From his phrasing it's impossible to tell whether he's addressing me as a man or a woman. Great! I reproach him, saying once again that I feel that I'm a woman in the same way that I feel the heat or cold.

'I want to be a woman. I am a woman…'

My friend, do you think it's healthy for me to be delving so deep into this reservoir of desires and intuitions? The psychoanalyst insists that this is the only way I can prepare myself properly for surgery.

Anyway, have I told you that that I finish my Fine Arts degree this year? Lots of us are really dreading it because we don't know what comes next. Father told me that he'd carry on supporting me for a year after the degree, and then that would be that. But, ever the sensible one, he's written me a letter of introduction to a sculptor friend of his who trained under many well-respected sculptors. I'm happy to work with him in any capacity: carving stone, modelling, working clay, whatever will earn me some money and help me to learn the profession.

At university I've had all kind of lecturers, some conservative who advised us to follow set paradigms; others really progressive, who would say that Fine Arts is a pointless degree because art is a language unique to each individual, a special way of reading reality, and the way other artists have gone about it is done, finished, and imitating them would be plagiarism. They said that our own work should prioritise originality and novelty. One in particular used to say, with majestic calm, that art is a dissident force, a personal attempt to transform society, a kind of constant revolution through one's work. I was particularly struck by one thing he said, that the truth of art lies in its capacity to lay to ruin the monopoly of so-called reality established by the majority. Yes! It is up to me to shape the hegemony of my concrete existence from my own body and my own desires. I don't know if others will help me in this, but art at least will be my ally.

Please forgive my digressions. I'm embarrassed because I'm aware that you know exactly what I'm talking about.

Be well.
Ruth

Dear friend,

I've been desperate to pin down an identity for my sexuality, and my sister suggests that I should try masturbation. This takes me by surprise. I confess that all the information I have about autoeroticism is male focussed, so much so that I need enlightening about female masturbation. I asked the psychoanalyst to teach me, and am amazed at what he has to say.

First, he gives me what amounts to a theory class on how the autoerotic instinct is directed not towards other people, but towards our own body. He explains that with this impulse the origin and objective are the same subject, and therefore everything is present in a closed circuit, whether the activity involves mouth, anus, vagina or breasts. As he speaks, I run my hand over my chest and explore between my legs and wonder how I might feel my vagina or breasts aroused if I don't have either. Regardless, I try stroking my penis – rub, caress, fondle, everything, and even turn to face a mirror so that I can see it more clearly. I realise that my penis isn't moving from its pinched, flaccid state. Then I try stimulating my anus but feel repelled, take hold of my mini-dick, and fail again. I have to accept that I don't have the ability to masturbate, that my body isn't responsive to my own demand.

I wonder why I felt so good with Raül, so aroused and orgasmic. What was my demand, and what was the nature of his supply? What's the difference between being me with myself and being me with him? Am I impenetrable to my own desire, but vulnerable to the desire of a man? Have I built a defensive barrier from fear of seeing deeper inside myself through masturbation, as though it were capable of revealing hitherto unknown dimensions? My body is against me, rebellious, unreceptive to my requests, a territory deaf to my persuasion.

My sister suggests I ask Raül for help, but that's not the same. Can one person be masturbated by another? In any case that wouldn't be autoerotic but just another kind of sexual play. I'm not convinced. I arrange for Raül to come to the house, secretly intending to test the reactions of my penis.

When we're naked we kiss and caress each other as before, and when he's hard I ask him to go down on me. The poor boy tries everything but nothing happens. I'm crestfallen, although at least this confirms that my penis serves no purpose.

According to my sister, I ought to be able to orgasm with my dick, diminutive though it is, because it equates an external clitoris which reproduces the most intense sexual responses in most women. Penis or clitoris, my dangling remnant of flesh was completely passive. Once again I realised that my identity couldn't be tied wholly to sexuality. I feel like a woman, but I'm not a woman because there's this thing binding me to my male form, even though it always fails.

I speak to the psychoanalyst again. He tells me that I'm in too much of a rush, that it will take whatever time it takes, especially in my case. He doesn't exactly say that my sister is wrong, but points out that she is doubtless at one with herself, has a healthy constitution and is in good shape. Not that he's suggesting I'm ill, he qualifies gently, but rather someone who needs the most attentive care to achieve an appropriate personal physiognomy and overall aspect.

And then he asks:

'During arousal, how did you feel?'

'What do you mean?'

'Was there some obstacle getting in the way of you and yourself?'

'Me, I suppose, most obviously.'

'And no-one else?'

'I can't remember.'

'Relax and cast your mind back. Let that situation take hold of you as if there is no material substance, as if you are not alone on the stage, and admit that perhaps there is, in fact, someone else who constitutes the real obstacle to you fulfilling yourself; live that act, relive it, all of it, intensely, without thinking, as though you're being carried by a gust of wind…'

'Mother! It's fucking mother!'

There's absolute silence. My heart is racing.

'Sorry?'

'My mother...'

With this revelation, he adopts a professional – by which I mean formal – tone, and summarises as follows:

'That presence could be interpreted on your part as envy of your mother's vagina.'

'Could you repeat that please?'

'Vagina envy. Your mother's vagina.'

'No way!'

He lets me shout and vent my horror. When I've calmed down, he says:

'The way your defences went up means that your mother is very problematic in all of this.'

'We've already talked about mother as a problem.'

'But now we have to pin down the details.'

'Meaning?'

'Meaning that this is not just about her accepting you as a male; you want to be for yourself like her vagina, in as much as the vagina is the supreme representation of your genital sexuality.'

'Envy my mother when I detest her, renounce her?'

'That is exactly why she constitutes a disturbance for you.'

I lose it, hurl insults, even swear. He doesn't interrupt. Then I burst into tears and, struggling to get my words out, try to say that if this envy is real, I will stop my treatment. He takes my hand very gently and says:

'Life often sets us predicaments that can look insurmountable. You don't have to stop anything. But I advise you to be prudent. The inside of us is often empty, and then sometimes, we don't know why, it fills up with images that make us uncomfortable. Don't think about fighting them, accept them as a fact that is no more important than you choose to it to be. Be careful with your erotic experiments because they could damage you. Avoid situations that might be advantageous to some but not everyone. Just as your body isn't the same, your sexuality is also differentiated. And your vital energy, what we call spirit, psyche or soul, is also not the same. This energy is the richest, most important part of you, and it's essential we protect it from harm.'

I feel like saying it's no big deal, but I hold my tongue because I know he's right.

Every day my breasts are a little more impressive, bigger, and when I look in the mirror I feel very satisfied. Raül notices and congratulates me. Why is Raül interested? Will we still be lovers? As the hormones take effect, perhaps love will start to look different to me.

I'll say goodbye now. My poor father's paying a regular allowance into the new bank account for me. It's his way of saying that he's there if I need him. I'll tell you about my father's sculptor friend next time. I'm living alone.

Take care.
Ruth

My dear friend,

I have really fond memories of my Fine Arts degree, and especially of lectures on the avantgardes. The professor used to emphasize that the avantgarde isn't a fashion that holds sway at a particular point in time but is a way of understanding and practising the creative act. I know that this is your area, and I'm talking about it because I want you to see that I haven't been wasting my time. What most interests me about the avantgardes is that they are transgressive, they violate social norms, fracture the repetitive burden of tradition, stand opposed to their moment in society, and ultimately incite the subject to rebel against collective uniformity. I felt instinctively at home with these principles because they helped me to realise that as an individual, I am increasingly differentiated from other people who wave the flag of 'normal'. Or am I? My insecurity will be no surprise if you recall that I affirmed my female condition very early on and proclaimed it fiercely, whereas now I have doubts. My friend, please don't forget that I'm in the middle of a process of transition, or perhaps of setting in order this profound disorder of my self. At this moment I don't think I can be faithful to anything outside of this change, this evolution.

I introduce myself to the sculptor my father recommended to me. He is still young, and when he reads my father's letter, he can't do enough for me. First, he asks about my studies and we talk about my vocation. Then he shows me his workshop. I am pleasantly surprised both by him and his work.

'What would you like to do?' he asks, out of the blue. When I don't answer, he adds: 'Come with me for now, and you can help me out.'

He leads me through to his studio, his touch on my shoulder conveying a friendly warmth. The work of this artist is a pendulum swinging from figurative expressionism to the most singular abstraction. Women are an almost ever-present theme, worn-down women who have had to bear the not always pleasant weight of life. Tired women who seem about to resign from life at any moment. And something that really catches my attention is the rural character of these women, most of them countryfolk.

'Who are all these women in your work?'

'I'm a son of the land, of the territories to the west. I grew up in a very poor, little village and lived there until my father threw me out to earn a living. I worked as a carpenter for a few years, and then as a cabinetmaker, until I was able to find work in the studios of well-known artists.'

Alongside these women, I marvel at his abstract and informal work, its cheerful lyricism and contagious optimism. I need to know how it's possible for the same artist to bring together two such distinct ways of understanding art.

'When it comes to it, there's really only one way of reading reality, the reading that begins and ends inside the artist. In other words, the style by which we externalise the configuration that has become established within us (the inside out) as a result of seeing the outside in, over and over. It's the style that's important, because everything else is set in stone way back… Style and its polymorphisms, its versatility. A person is never the same because the life of the subject is polyvalent and mutable. A person who is always the same to herself is already dead. Life is the seduction of change…'

The sculptor's workshop is a huge space where he works wood, clay and stone, and where he combines objects which signify plurality in order to achieve a final unity. Found objects removed from their context and reconfigured, sometimes with a strong surrealist twist. It's this force that attracts me, this free association that I practise sometimes when I see the psychoanalyst: an uncensored discourse that allows me to see what emerges from within.

Before I leave he offers me a glass of wine. As we drink, he studies me closely and then remarks on my feminine beauty.

'You're a very pretty girl. Would you like to model for me?' I'm not expecting this request because the women in his work, as I've said, tend to be older with weather-worn complexions. Before I have chance to say anything, he orders, rather than asks: 'Take off your clothes.'

I obey mechanically, perhaps because I've gotten used to undressing. Once naked, he helps me onto a small pedestal. He takes a few steps back and studies me thoughtfully. He shouts:

'Incredible!' And then: 'A man-woman… A perfect ephebe… It's all there.' He comes closer to examine me. 'Two wondrous breasts and a little dick that's embryonic of every dick in the world. That's just how forms should be: suggested, insinuated, hinted at, only teasingly evident.' He pauses as though choosing his words, and then exclaims loudly: 'You are perfect! Always preserve this perfection that the gods have favoured you with, because you are the daughter of gods, not of men. A man and a woman together could never procreate such excellence…'

Amid a paroxysm of wonderment, he kisses my feet with almost reverential adoration. Such delirious exultation both disconcerts and pleases me, because it bolsters my internal equilibrium, freeing me from the potential ugliness of error. I, my body, my desire, my will are aligned with human perfection. He said it, the sculptor, in a mad, epiphanic moment.

At the studio door he tells me that he wants me to model for his next piece.

'I'm going to leave the world-weary women and instead sculpt the harmony that nature on rare occasions presents to us. I'm going to make you the symbol of all human languages, convert you into the exultation of what you already are: the serene diction of beauty, a proclamation of the pure body against the foul social body. Men and women are ephemeral because life drains them. Only people like you are above life and its servitude.' And just when I think he's finished, he sentences: 'Heterodoxy alone is a worthy consort of art.'

Wow! I was overwhelmed but also excited by the visit, one of those encounters that disrupts routine and its shortcomings, and hands you an intriguing challenge when you're least expecting it. There are no invitations, because the only people who count are those capable, either by chance or necessity, of shattering the stultifying horizons.

Enough, I don't want to bore you. Just let me say that everything seems to be coming together for me. Perhaps I'll carry on believing it while the inertia of my meeting with father's sculptor friend lasts. Art, consort of my destiny.

Be well.
Ruth

My friend,

I met up with my sister's friends and Raül, who was very charming. We went to a club, but there was too much noise and too many people. Curiously Raül's presence feels less immediate than before, more indifferent, and my sister's friends don't hold the same interest for me either.

I decide to go to the Registry Office to change my name and am welcomed by an extremely unattractive woman who looks me up and down. She addresses me informally.

'Why do you want to change your name?'

'And why are you treating me with so little respect?'

She seems disconcerted.

'What are your grounds?'

'Whatever the grounds, they're absolutely no business of yours. The day I was born they needed no grounds to register my name here; they simply informed you I'd been born. Now I've been reborn and I want to be known as Ruth, okay?'

The registrar doesn't have a clue what's going on. 'You'll have to apply in writing.'

'Rubbish! Here, my exemption.' I hand her a copy of my military certificate.

'That's no good to me.'

Then I lose my patience, unbutton my blouse and show her my breasts. Astonished, she asks me for my identity card and studies it closely. 'It says Raül.'

'Precisely, Madam, what a genius you are. And from now on it needs to say Ruth.'

'And is there a Saint Ruth?'

'Saints days, chamber pots! As if they're relevant anymore.'

She opens a filing cabinet and takes out my record. She reads, picks up a fountain pen and in one of the margins writes that from this day forth it is the will of the undersigned that I be known as Ruth, rather than Raül.

'Great. Now I'd like a document certifying the change so that I can give it to the police, and they'll understand without my having to go into endless detail.'

She doesn't object, and still hasn't recovered herself when I make my way out with the document in hand. Outside, I burst into violent laughter.

Oh my friend, where on earth did that authoritarian rush come from? I'm sure when I first set eyes on that ugly old pen-pusher I drew courage from my youthful good looks, as validated by the sculptor. I'd misused them, but they were my power after all. I go to the police station too and have to queue at window number 1. When my turn comes, I suddenly feel tired.

'I'd like to update my identity card.'

'Why?'

'Because my first name needs changing.'

'Why?'

I hand over the military exemption certificate and the Civil Registry document.

'You'll need to go to window number 3.'

The policeman I've spoken to is a young man who undresses me with his eyes. As I join the other queue, he calls to his colleague at the window and shouts: 'Got a queer for you!'

My legs are trembling. I turn round and go back to window number 1. I stand square in front of the first policeman and almost shriek: 'Either take back what you just said or I'll report you to your superior.'

'You can't be soliciting here, love. Take it as it comes or get out.'

'How dare…! I demand respect.'

I'm really screaming now, my legs are shaking and my mouth's dry. I don't know where I learned to be so vulgar, but I yell at him: 'I'd rip your balls off if you had any, dickhead!'

He counters, and I have another go at him, and we're making such a racket that an inspector comes to investigate.

'What's the matter, Miss?'

'Your officer here has insulted me and treated me with utter contempt.'

The inspector must be about fifty years old.

'Would you like to come with me, Miss?' He takes me to his office and offers me a seat. Sitting down opposite, he says: 'Every citizen should be able to assert their rights, Miss, but you have to acknowledge that it's bound to cause a stir when a young, attractive woman like you has a man's name.'

His tone reassures me, and I hand over the two documents. He reads them and picks up the phone to ask another policeman to come in. The inspector instructs him to fill in a specific form, and return it once completed.

'Are you having a rough time of it, Miss Ivars, Ruth – if I may?'

I mull over my answer. 'I'm not the only one who has problems; I'd say lots of men aren't clear about how their own sexuality fits together, both inside and outside society, as though both public and private spaces are the exclusive dominion of males who have carte blanche to trample on female citizens like animals in the wild…'

The inspector interrupts me to ask: 'What did you study at university?'

'Fine Arts.'

'You don't seem to have changed your name on a whim.'

'That's right, I haven't. It was a necessity in the context of a sensitive personal situation which has nothing to do with any kind of perversion.'

'And once you're called Ruth, what are your plans?'

'At the moment I want to be able to deal with those unpleasant situations when I'm asked for documentation. The immediate problem is my degree certificate: I need it to say Ruth.'

'And which of the visual arts do you intend specialising in, Ruth?'

'Sculpture.'

'Sculpture?'

'I already have a workshop.'

He takes out a business card and gives it to me. 'Can I have an invitation to your first exhibition?'

The officer comes back in with the completed form and the inspector makes a photocopy: 'Your new identity card will be ready in about two weeks' time. Come straight through to my office.'

My sister reminds me that I'll have to take my new identity card to the curial office so that my name can be changed in the baptismal record. 'Why?' I ask. 'So that your name is consistent everywhere.'

Two weeks later I go to the police station to collect my card. The inspector isn't there, but a courteous, softly spoken sergeant helps me. As he hands me the new card, he says:

'Could I ask you something, Miss Ruth?'

'Please do.'

'Are there many cases out there like yours? We hadn't come across any before; you were the first. Perhaps not everyone is as scrupulous as you. A lot of people live with the ambiguity of their situation; not everyone is as intelligent, and it's common for people to get involved in prostitution, of all kinds.'

He accompanies me to the door. We pass the police officer who caused all the commotion last time, at window number 1. When he sees me he stands up and apologises to me as I half laugh and wave goodbye.

With the new identity card in my bag, I head for the curial office. I'm made to wait a good while in a bare, empty room before I'm invited into an office where a priest sits in his robes. I explain why I've come, and he looks at me like I'm an idiot, and says:

'That's impossible.'

'Why?'

'Because you'll always be Raül.'

'What the hell…!' I am requesting you to alter my name.'

He searches for my baptismal record in a huge ledger.

'It states quite clearly here that you were baptised Raül, and as a sacrament, baptism imprints character, an indelible spiritual mark.'

'What does that mean?'

'It means that you are a Christian man, and you can never be a

Christian woman.'

'Let's start at the beginning: if I was baptised, it was without my knowledge; I was made a Christian without my consent, and so this whole ceremony that you call baptism is invalid.'

The priest was visibly livid and was about to come back at me, but I cut him off and added vigorously:

'Since I did not consent, I am not baptised. Therefore, as of today, I consider myself removed from the baptismal register, and if one day I want to become involved in religion, I will formally and consciously make that move myself. You can't take advantage of children like this, it's an abuse of people's freedom.'

I get up to leave, but am stopped by the priest's words: 'You're speaking gibberish, you're obviously not well. The devil's in you, just look how you're dressed, Mr Raül Ivars...'

'What about you? You're dressed like a eunuch, clearly.'

And I flounce out.

My friend, am I getting more aggressive? I used to be quiet, calm, but I'm now so volatile. Is my personality raging out of control? When everything's finally resolved, will my good nature return? I suspect it's the behaviour of the authorities that is pushing me to breaking point. Could they be more compassionate? I'll have to talk to the psychoanalyst and see how he interprets it. I'm regretting now being so hard on the priest, but behind this coarse outer there's a truth that will not be denied. Anyway, why would I want a birth certificate with my new name on it? It's not as though I want to get married, hell no! Although I wouldn't be the first transsexual to be married in Church either.

Now I just have to go into university to ask them to make out the degree certificate to say 'Ruth'. I don't think there'll be any problems because the administration, my lecturers, and my fellow students all know me by my female name.

I hope we'll soon see the end of this ritual of confusion.

Take care.
Ruth

Letter 10

My friend,

My identity documents and my degree certificate now say 'Ruth'. And, as you know, I've been exempted from military service. I update my psychoanalyst and tell him that I'm now legally a woman. No-one can now question my female condition... except in bed. My appearance is perfectly female, my taste in clothes is tastefully feminine, and everyone from now on, even mother, will call me Ruth.

The psychoanalyst advises me to start getting used to the idea that my surgery will happen soon, but to do so calmly, without melodrama.

'The whole team is in place: the surgeon, gynaecologist, sexologist, neurologist, endocrinologist, the clinic, and the analysts. It seems to me that you've done the mental work, and managed to update your identity in society sufficiently, to be able to withstand an operation of this kind.'

I explain that I'd like to be able to meet the surgeon. He agrees, and in fact letters of introduction for each of the specialists he's lined up are already typed out. I visit the surgeon first.

Two nurses greet me. One takes my family details and asks a few insignificant questions. The other shows me through to an empty waiting room and then leaves me. A few minutes later she's back, and we go into the doctor's consulting room. As far as I can see the whole building is decorated very soberly in light colours, almost white. The surgeon gets to his feet to welcome me and invites me to take a seat. He's mature, has white hair and a tidy white beard, and is wearing a white lab coat. He sits down next to me. His eyes are dull and everything about him smells clean. He asks me to tell my story and listens attentively. When he thinks he's heard enough, he picks up the phone and calls through to one of the two nurses. When she arrives, he asks her to help me undress, completely. Naked again! He examines me as I stand in front of him, and then as I lie on the exam table. When he's finished, I get dressed and we sit down again.

'I think we can be confident that surgery will be successful in your case. But I'll speak to the gynaecologist once he's seen you.'

'What will my female sex be like?' I ask straight out.

'We'll construct a vagina from the skin around your penis and from the penis itself. I'll shrink whatever prostate you have and make a female urethra.'

'And my vagina will allow me to have sexual intercourse?'

'Yes, completely.'

'And orgasms?'

'Female pleasure, my dear Ruth, isn't merely somatic, focussed on the body, but also psychic, emotional. If penetration happens as an act of love, pleasure is guaranteed. In the context of rape, for example, of forcible penetration, the male may experience pleasure but not the female.'

His description of the surgery is rose-tinted. I trust this man. Days later I visit the sexologist. His practice is in what looks like a squat. He answers the door himself and leads me into a small room where we sit on a sofa as though we're about to have tea and erudite conversation. There's no lab coat; instead, he's wearing a thick turtle-neck jumper and flannel trousers. Once again I recount my story, almost mechanically now. He's aware I'm on autopilot and interrupts me from time to time to ask questions. When he thinks he has a grasp of the details, he jumps to his feet and paces around the room. All of a sudden, he stops right in front of me and asks, 'Why do you want surgery, lad?'

'To be a complete woman.'

'And why do you want to be a woman?'

'Because I feel like a woman.'

'How long have you felt like this?'

'Since I was a small child.'

'So you wouldn't say it's a choice?'

'No.'

'Ok, and you want them to cut it off?' The question is as grubby as the surroundings. I'm not sure what to say.

'Yes, it's not good for anything. I want a vagina.'

'Are you choosing a vagina, or do you need a vagina?'

'I need a vagina.'

'Why?'

'To complete my identity: legally I'm a woman.'

'What do you mean?'

'I'm registered as female with all the authorities.'

And now…'

'… now I just need a vagina.'

'And why don't you accept who you already are?'

'Because I don't feel like myself.'

'But that "I" is who you are now, and after surgery, what do you think this "I" will be like? Will it change? Will you be the woman you imagine yourself to be in your head?'

'Enough!' I yell in his face, springing up off the sofa. He doesn't flinch, but looks at me, smiles, and asks me to sit down.

'Please calm down. We've got to be absolutely thorough, fella,' he says, adopting a tone of authority. 'Right now you're a misshapen man. What will you be afterwards?'

'They're confident I'll be a complete woman.'

'Complete?'

'With a vagina, my body will be complete. And my sense of self has been female for a long time.'

'Am I right in saying that you think the female condition rests uniquely on the presence of a vagina?'

'Yes.'

'But if you've felt yourself, and feel yourself, to be a woman before you have a vagina, that means the female condition as a reality exists without a vagina. That being the case, why do you need a vagina?'

'So I can be a complete woman, body and soul!' I scream.

'Since when is a woman's soul secondary to a vagina?' I bite my tongue to prevent another outburst. He can see what's happening.

'I'm not trying to torture you. I want to try to get you to realise that you're focussing the whole of your identity on your sex. Why do we want to be our sex before we're even people? Why don't we accept nature's successes and shortcomings and admit a spiritual hegemony over them? Why don't we take a look from time to time inside ourselves and report back on how we're configured? Why do we insist on wanting to choose? Why do we opt for an alien disguise rather than the physiognomy that's already ours? Why do we lay so little store by our intellect, and so much by our instincts? Why are we so submissive in the face of damaging social imperatives? Why can't we be gods…?'

There's a tense yet illuminating silence. I wonder who this doctor is: sexologist, moralist, quack? This interrogation reminds me of the conversation I had with Raül one day, and even of the questions I've asked myself. Why do I have to choose, why do I want to construct a complete woman? Because social pressure and paradigms force me to: I'm either a man, or a woman. And because I've always felt like a woman and I have the chance to be complete, which is what I want for myself. The social fabric and its order do not admit ambiguities. As if he can see inside my head, the sexologist breaks the silence.

'It's quite true that society is uncomfortable with ambiguity because its security is founded on concrete knowledge of every person's identity and circumstance, and in society's name nature is prostituted to satisfy parameters which are strictly adhered to. Nobody escapes the levelling process…'

There's nothing left for us to say. The visit's over. At the door, he says:

'On the day of your surgery, I'll be at your side.'

When I get home, I start wondering what the sexologist's story is, where his opinions come from, what his ultra butch appearance is all about… Tomorrow we're going to the beach. It'll be my stage.

Be well.
Ruth

Dear friend,

I hear about a medium, psychic or fortune teller-type who's able to divine people's nature and identity. He lives in the old town in a huge old pile of a house. I knock on the door and he answers it himself. It's as though he's waiting for me, and he beckons for me to follow him to a little chapel decorated all over with eyes. There are eyes on the walls, ceiling, and even on the small, round table in the centre of the room. The light is soft and the air is fragrant with lavender. We sit opposite each other cross-legged on floor cushions. We've never seen each other before and we have no contacts in common. He's dressed in a sort of white tunic, and his head and face are close-shaven. His eyes are wide and dark. He has me lay my hands palm up on the little table and studies them before laying his own palms on top of mine. There's warmth. While we're touching, he stares intensely into my eyes, and I feel a luminous, immensely pleasurable sensation flow through me. He murmurs very deliberately and I am drawn to him

'Come closer, accept me, allow me to help you. Everything changes, everything transitions, everything passes... people's spirit, and their bodies,' he says, pausing with great effect before adding, 'Difference is beginning to make itself felt in you. You're a mutation; you are an example of how humanity initiates the process by which new human beings are made, beings who reproduce themselves by a kind of parthenogenesis or hermaphroditism which will wipe out our dependence on coupling and put an end to biological sex...'

It sounds as though this takes some effort to say, evidenced by the beads of sweat on his brow. He removes his hands from mine and waves them in the air like two flags. His gaze shifts in the same direction before he lets out something like a small howl.

'Welcome, young lady..., young man...,' he says, suddenly. 'Thank you for your visit.' And as though offering a diagnosis, he says very slowly, 'Outside of you there is nothing... the whole universe lives, and is as one, in you; you are you within difference; outside of this difference you would be lost in the toxic repetition of matter…'

Until this moment his face has been impassive. Now he smiles briefly, serenely, as if wanting to communicate an immense inner peace. Reassured by his calm, I return his smile.

'You are your own musical score, and there is no music but your own. You are the guardian of your rhythm, tempo, every beat. It's a silent score that will always live in you. Outside everything is noise, uproar, confusion, a babel of ferment. Yours is the sidereal harmony of everything-as-one and everything-as-nothing. The cosmos resides in you. You are beyond the objectification that attempts to transform things into myths that become snares and cages. You are the subject, the sovereign.'

I'm tired. He sees this and claps his hands. A young male – I think – enters, completely naked, and serves tea. I can't help but look him up and down. I can't take my eyes off him, and I realise he has neither breasts nor penis, is in fact neither male nor female. I'm perplexed. The medium interjects:

'You think you've seen what doesn't exist. Neither girl nor boy. Reality doesn't exist: everything is inside you. Nothing you see is real. We're alone and there's nothing to say you're visiting anyone. Outside of yourself, everything becomes illusory.'

If we include this conversation which, fantasies aside, really did take place, that's three people now who have interpreted me in a quite worrying way: the sculptor, the sexologist, and this charlatan. And at times perhaps the psychoanalyst too. There's a degree of overlap in what they've said, and this makes me very uneasy. Maybe because it's not a million miles from what I think myself when I have time to reflect calmly. I admit though that I'm enjoying meeting these people, or at least it's no hardship. My peculiarities get people talking. I'm done in today, though.

Be well.
Ruth

Letter 12

My friend,

As I mentioned to you, we went to the beach, and it was incredible. The water was cool, cold even, so we lay in the sun instead, and wandered along the shoreline. There were very few people around, so we set off to explore a neighbouring beach. It was full of naturists, and I was astonished to see so many naked people. My attention was drawn to the men with their bits hanging out. The older men were the most well-endowed, perhaps because, to paraphrase Lamarck, use makes the organ. There was much more variety amongst the younger men, including several indeterminate individuals who gave me the confidence to take off my swimsuit. I wasn't scared of looking ridiculous and, in fact, no-one seemed to notice me. Curiously those bathers understood nudity as completely normal and therefore also respected each other's privacy. It occurred to me that it's clothing rather than nudity itself that gives rise to scandal.

Every member of our group ended up naked, and there was some embarrassment, and perhaps for some, arousal. I mention it because two of the lads got erections and literally had to take the plunge to sort it out. My sister and one of her girlfriends waded out with them and there ensued a kind of erotic play-fight that was barely concealed by the waves. I envied them a little, and perhaps if Raül had been there, we'd have joined them, albeit limited somewhat by my singularity.

I decided to take a walk instead, fascinated by the penises that seemed to be competing in all their infinite variety. I was struck by the fact that the more corpulent men with rounded bellies had smaller dicks, sometimes so insignificant that they were barely visible between their thighs amid a thicket of pubic hair. By contrast, the more lanky, even scrawny types tended to be extremely well-endowed and quite a sight, especially to those of us unaccustomed to such generous proportions. Arses were another matter, however: the skinnier men's buttocks were ugly, while the big men showed theirs off with a certain swagger. I have no complaints about mine, they're shapely and well-proportioned.

But I'll admit to a gnawing penis envy. This remnant of masculinity I am still stuck with gave me a kind of impostor syndrome in that context, and I felt my body hijacked. I have proclaimed myself a woman over and over to every authority in existence and any yet to be. On the nudist beach that day my penis envy was real, and I cursed nature for having endowed me so cruelly. When I said 'nature' I thought about my evil mother who had conceived me and who bore me incomplete, unable to act on my desires.

Let me finish telling you about the beach. Still walking, I headed for some rocks and came across a young man and woman making love. It was the first love scene I'd witnessed in real life. Two beautiful bodies unified, finding themselves in each other, oblivious to my presence. After they climaxed, they saw me. He was lying spent on the sand, but she turned to me with a laugh that seemed welcoming. She motioned for me to come over.

'Here kid, make me happy…'

The sand swallowed my feet and I couldn't move. She got to her feet and made her way to me instead, knelt in front of me and gasped with surprise.

'What a pretty little thing…!'

She kissed me, licked me, and took me into her mouth eagerly, but when she realised I was still flaccid, she pulled away with a frown.

I said it was the first time I'd seen a couple making love. That's not quite true, because one summer evening I'd caught mother and father having sex. They were naked on the bed grappling, which seemed to me a wholly indecent exhibition of two unattractive bodies ruined by age. I'd often heard my parents argue, sometimes violently, but I'd never seen them shagging, panting like caged beasts. It looked as though it was her, mother, who was taking the lead energetically, almost to the point, one might have said, of wanting to rip off father's penis. To keep it for herself? When he penetrated her, whose dick was it? Who was putting father into mother? Was she being fucked or was she fucking? For a long time afterwards I imagined mother as possessing a sceptre that made her sovereign of a power not rightly hers, but which reinforced her authority regardless. Perhaps that fantasy still lingers. The psychoanalyst says that this might be the single most important cause of my lack of acceptance of mother. Up to this point I've always thought of myself as someone who can't be penetrated, and so as incapable of being invested with the mark of power that the phallus bestows. In whatever degree, I have a penis. So why should I wish to receive one from outside of myself? After surgery everything'll be different because the congenital aberration will be erased and enthroned in its place will be the true sceptre, to be realised fully by the seduction of the best male. This is my destiny: to be fully a woman, to be replenished with power at each penetration.

I'm not talking nonsense, my friend, although you'd be forgiven for thinking so. My life is dominated obsessively by this labyrinth of contemplation I find myself in. Will I find a way out? At times I feel paralysed by so many turns, going over and over the past in my mind, reflecting on the present and yet unable to see clearly what the future might hold. Is it so difficult to be a woman? Is there such a high price to pay?

Please forgive me if my writing gets repetitive. Be patient with me, because every letter brings some relief and new strength to make it to the end. And yes, once or twice I've thought about giving up, even about suicide to rid myself of this wretched body and all the noise around it that makes me think, feel and say such abnormal things. I'm sorry.

Take care.
Ruth

Dear friend,

I've started work with my father's friend, the sculptor. I'm modelling for him, as he suggested when I first visited. Once I'm naked, he poses me on the same pedestal as before and studies me from afar, then close up, moves my legs apart and lifts my arms in the air.

'Relax, I don't want you stiff and awkward. Stand as though you've just been for a quick walk and you're neither tired nor surprised to have made it back.' He pauses before then saying, 'Your expression needs to tell me that you're aware you don't have a body, as though your corporeal form were an intangible, incorporeal essence.'

I understand what he means and try to do as he says.

'Now, don't move.'

And from a few paces away he begins to sketch me from different angles. One sheet of paper, two, three... and five in the end.

'Take a break now, come and sit on my lap. I need to get a sense of your weight.'

I obey.

'Sculptures need to have a certain heft, but they should also seem to fly. You are incredibly beautiful! You have the serenity I have always sought for my work: to be and not to be in time, to be and not to be in form, to be and not to be in existence...'

He strokes my skin softly as though he wants to perceive the warmth and vibration of the infinite pulses that oscillate through it.

The study is now devoid of any references to his previous work, as though he is just starting out, and I am the first model he's had sit for him. There is absolutely nothing here. Reading my mind, he says:

'Art is always its own succession, and everything continues because everything is rediscovered.'

I climb onto the pedestal again, and he walks around me, still talking.

'There is always an aesthetic rupture because there is social rupture when the monopoly of established reality is broken. The old isn't better simply because it's old, and the same goes for the new. And whatever veneer dealers give to art, it continues to be a dissident force that emerges from content converted into form. You will be the content that I will convert into form. I will make you as I see you internalised within me.' He is still talking as he takes off his clothes and stands naked before me. 'You can get down.'

Then he climbs onto the pedestal in my place. As I said, he's still a young man, and looks even younger unclothed. I examine him with enthusiastic curiosity from all angles. I am drawn to his muscular buttocks and, from the other side, his handsome penis and impressive testicles. And I wonder why I don't have testicles, not even a trace. Are they lost, suspended in some pregenital stage? Perhaps the day they construct my vagina they'll find them asleep in the cradle of the epididymis, shying away from the challenge of being male or female. As I stand before this man, I am surer than ever that I am nothing close to being a man, and can only possibly be a woman. He gets down from the pedestal and comes over to me. He takes my hand and places it on his penis. I grasp it and look at the sculptor.

'How do you feel?' he asks. 'Do you sense any kind of communication with me? I mean, do you recognize that this is where my art comes from?'

I'm taken aback. Seeing this, he grabs hold of my mini dick and grazes my lips with a kiss. We walk around the studio with our arms around each other and stop in front of the bench where he left the sketches. I can't get over his skill and artistry.

'These drawings will help me to transform you in clay.'

'So I won't need to be here anymore?'

'You will, because you have to learn the profession, the techniques.' We agree I'll return at five the following afternoon. I'd like to discuss all of this with the psychoanalyst; I'm sure he'll have something to say.

The sculptor's theories about art are interesting, entertaining even. However, I'm not convinced that the mutual holding of dicks to bring about aesthetic communication makes any sense to me. At the same time, if I'm honest, I feel very much at ease with this artist. Does he mean that art is an erotics? Is he trying to say that between him and I there can never be physical love… in a normal way? Or that only in the illusion of possibility can things become clear, that is, how they are capable of being? And that in this illusion or fiction lies the truth of everyday reality? I think I'll go back to see the sexologist to see if he can help me process this.

I don't know what kind of trigger has brought to mind something my father said, along the lines of 'what's done can't be undone, and what's gone can't be recovered'. He also used to say, 'if you choose, you lose'. Perhaps I should have listened to him more. But was he saying these things for my benefit, or ruminating out loud thinking that no-one would hear? I want to get drunk.

Be well.
Ruth

Letter 14

My friend,

I've been going to the sculptor's workshop for a number of days now. I've seen how the clay is transformed, matching me in symmetry. Symmetry though, not calque. It's very pleasing to see the fingers of the master at work, adding clay and scraping it away from different parts of this mass which is gradually starting to resemble me. After a couple of weeks the piece looks finished, but he continues to remodel it as though searching for aspects beyond the physical lines he has already moulded.

'I want it to be you as you are inside as well as outside,' he says, repeatedly. 'I want the clay to express the contradiction that is present in you, the doubt-fuelled anxiety that drives you. When I'm happy that the clay has captured you completely, the marble will then celebrate your identity: it'll be patient work that might take months. You'll need to be here every day. It's important I have you close by, to feel the eloquence of your skin, shaped by the internal force striving to get out.'

I don't dare tell him that he won't see me for a couple of months because of the surgery and post-op treatment. I won't be able to write to you either.

I'm feeling nervous about things in spite of the fact that all the specialists involved have assured me that there's no reason the surgery shouldn't be completely successful. Perhaps I'm uncertain because this was a choice, an act of freedom that I alone am responsible for; and I can't know whether it'll work out for me or not. It's not some arbitrary act but something I have consciously researched, reconciled myself to, and set in motion, independently of social or family pressure, an act of free will, a right I am exercising from my place of solitude. With this freedom I opt to brutalize my body, forcibly mould it to the shape of the femininity that I live as an internal reality, not as a fairy tale or phantasm. I've talked to you many times about this, but please let me do so again, to see if I can overcome this anxiety. I know you can't do anything to help, but just writing it down helps to calm me. My friend, you know that what I want from all this is to experience love fully, to be able to love passionately with a woman's desire. I've been having hormone injections for months, as prescribed by the surgeon. My breasts are fuller (I've beaten my body!), and now there's just the big commitment remaining, the life-changer. If all goes well, I'll be going into hospital next Monday.

I've also written to my father to tell him that I have a date for surgery and to let him know how much it'll cost. I think he'll be true to form and help out financially. I've also told my sister and Raül, and said that I don't want any visitors; I'll see them when it's all over. I sent my mother a letter in the following terms: 'I'm not having it cut off, but re-ordering my anatomy so that I can be a normal woman. I'm not a man who wants to be a woman, but a woman with the wrong attributes, and these need correcting. I have a woman's brain, and it's my brain that generates my female sense of self.' And a few other things, but I kept it short, because I find it distressing to go over this again and again.

So everything is planned out, and the specialists say that it'll go well. One more reflection, though: I know that the clitoris has no reproductive role and that its function is sexual arousal and pleasure. But if my new clitoris is constructed from my existing penis, how will it be possible for me to experience pleasure if my penis has never given me any pleasurable sensation? Am I going to end up being a pleasure void? If my 'male' member doesn't function as it should and has never been able to give me male enjoyment, will I be able to orgasm as a woman when it is converted into a clitoris?

Every member of my case team, whether still involved or not, has said repeatedly that I will experience pleasure. I suspect however, as the surgeon intimated, that this pleasure is likely to be vaginal, because my new vagina will allow me to have benign sexual relations. I see a greater possibility of success here, but I won't know until I'm penetrated by a male.

My friend, it's excruciating to think that my future as a woman might only be enlightened by penetration. That my whole raison d'être is reduced to coitus. Doesn't this seem too biological to you, that I'm headed inexorably towards an irrational, reductive servitude? I almost said too animal. Perhaps intercourse will fail at first but be more rewarding thereafter. I'll need to choose the right man, and we'll need to take our time to learn what's possible. I consider Raül straight away because I think he'd be the ideal person; we've already been together more than once and he knows who I am and who I can be very well. I also wonder about my father's sculptor friend but decide against him because he has so many preconceptions about my identity. He probably wouldn't work for me.

My dear friend, please think of me. If anyone is to visit, it should surely be you, but no, I don't want visitors. I'll write again when it's over.

Be well.
Ruth

PART TWO
(*Acquired Situation*)

Letter 15

Dear friend,

It's all done. I'll explain the process to you so that you get an idea of what's been going on. Before the whole ritual of transformation begins, a nurse presents me with a consent form that says something like 'I, the undersigned... identity card number... date of birth... home address... authorize Dr... to carry out male-to-female gender reassignment surgery, understanding that complications may arise from this procedure... Please sign here.'

I read the form twice and then sign.

'Everything will be fine, but surgery can be...'

I've made the choice of my own free will, I've taken the risks on board, and I understand that the surgeon wants to cover his back. Medicine is a long way from being an exact science, and the patient must realise that mistakes happen. But I'm still surprised when the nurse asks me for the contact details of my next of kin. I'm not expecting that. It stops me cold. I give her my sister's name and address. That final step completed, she asks me to settle the invoice for all treatment and services at reception. I have the funds in place.

The night before they carry out a series of tests. A nurse takes me to a room, helps me undress, gives me a hospital gown and sits me on the bed. She leaves, and shortly after another girl comes in. She washes my pubic area and shaves me. When I realise that I don't have a single hair remaining, I'm overcome by a sense of naked vulnerability. I ask for a mirror so that I can see myself properly and imprint a last image of my genital confusion. I think, you've been with me for so many years only to end up under the implacable law of the scalpel.

A young man comes in, takes my blood pressure, listens to my chest and shines a torch into my eyes. Then he gives me an injection.

'This is a pre-anaesthetic sedative. It'll help you to get a good night's sleep. Know that it'll all go well, that you're in the hands of the best surgeon.'

I don't sleep though, I'm just very drowsy. The room fills with orderlies and nurses. They give me another injection and have me urinate. I piss as though I'm saying goodbye to my last male bond, almost with a sense of bereavement… They help me onto a trolley attended by male nurses. I hear them say that they might ask the surgeon to save them my dick instead of it ending up in the anatomical waste. Although I'm only semi-conscious, the comment makes an impression, and I even find it slightly hurtful. The surgeon is waiting for me at the doors to the operating theatre and greets me very warmly. He's fresh-faced, attractive.

'I know you're still awake enough to hear me. You are very beautiful. Have faith in me: in two or three hours it'll all be over. Your body and mind are in perfect condition.'

I'm lifted across onto the operating table, and they intubate. Then I stop hearing myself.

If I lose consciousness gradually, enveloped in fog, now I come round quite briskly.

'That's it, you're waking up. Everything's fine.'

I think they say that I was under for about three hours. Now I hear the surgeon's voice:

'I couldn't have wished for a better subject. It's been a pleasure to work on you.'

'You make a very pretty girl,' someone adds, 'very pleasing on the eye…'

I'm sufficiently alert to realise I'm back in my room. When I've come round completely, the surgeon pays me a visit.

'I wanted to thank you for helping everything go so smoothly, and for such a gift of a body. This is the best procedure I've ever carried out. A colleague recorded it on video and when you're completely recovered, you'll be able to watch it. I would love to be able to show it at a conference, with your consent, of course. I'll leave you to rest now, Ruth. We'll see each other tomorrow.'

I have a good night. Mid-morning, the surgeon arrives without his white coat, wearing a navy-blue blazer, grey flannel trousers, sky blue shirt and a yellow tie bearing what look like modernista squiggles: he looks very elegant. He inspects my wounds with a delicate, practised touch.

'Splendid.'

He covers me again, and kisses my forehead, the first kiss I receive from a man as a whole woman. I smile faintly in thanks.

'I'll leave you in the charge of my assistant, and we'll see each other again when it's time to take the stitches out.'

Hygiene, fruit juice, soft food. I want to pee. One of the nurses I've met before comes to help. This is the first time I've urinated as a woman. There's no discomfort at all, as though this is always how I've peed, and the nurses around me seem reassured.

'Is there anything you need?'

'I'm thirsty.'

In the afternoon, I'm visited by the psychoanalyst, sexologist, and neurologist in quick succession. The first is very pleased. 'Once you're back on your feet, we've got a lot of work to do,' he says. He's not here long. Then the sexologist, and neurologist, in turn. I feel looked after, protected, but I'd like to be alone and have time to think. The gynaecologist comes the next day. A week later I'm discharged and sent home. My sister has prepared my room.

'You look well, and your colour's good. The fridge is fully stocked.'

'I need a change of clothes.'

When I'm undressed, I realise my sister's desperate to see the results of the operation. I lie down on the bed with my legs open so that she can see my new sex. She puts her face up close to the wound quite brazenly, and scrutinizes it.

'Incredible, it's real! When your hair grows back, it'll look just like mine.'

I put on my best lingerie with meticulous attention, as if I'm dressing a virgin. For the first time ever I don't feel like it's some form of costume. I pick out a short kilt and white blouse and match them with understated stockings and shoes. My sister suggests that I should get my hair done professionally, but until then, she's going to style it for me.

'You've gone a shade lighter; it suits you. They say the anaesthetic does that.'

All of this is prologue to my premiere. This is my first letter to you from the other side of the border, from my new life. I don't feel able to go and see my parents yet, but I know it has to be done, and quite soon, if only to thank my father who has been so generous. My mother's another story, and I sense real difficulty there. It'll be a huge blow for her, and I'll need to prepare thoroughly.

That's all for now. I hope you're well.
Ruth

Letter 16

My friend,

I go to have my stitches out, and I don't feel a thing. It's the same surgeon, and he congratulates me on the sex that he himself has created for me.

'It seems to be settling down nicely, and you'll be able to make love as a woman now. But avoid rough sex, and use lubricant. You will experience a pleasurable sensation, and you'll have fun, provided that there's an emotional connection with your partner. You can't have children, obviously; your sex is for love, not procreation. Being a woman isn't necessarily about having children, but about knowing what it is to be a woman, how to behave, feel, think, live the feminine and, not so much, perhaps, the female. You'll be very happy, Ruth, because you have a huge capacity for love and acceptance.'

He says many more things, I'm sure, but these words are engraved on my brain and I will never forget them. Buoyed by a sense of victory and with renewed optimism, I arrange to see the psychoanalyst. He's been informed of my progress and congratulates me.

'How are you feeling, Miss Ivars?' His smile seems oddly sly and it catches me off guard.

'I feel well, happy, satisfied, triumphant even...'

'Have you decided what to do about your mother?'

'I know I have to go to see her, and I will, with the confidence that there is common ground, as one woman to another, one vagina to another, one clitoris.'

'It's quite possible that your mother will accuse you of being half a woman because you can't have children, and are therefore sterile. As the surgeon and gynaecologist have undoubtedly explained, the surgery doesn't extend to procreation; we can't improvise wombs.'

'I don't give a damn about motherhood; I don't want to be a mother. It's a function of femaleness that I've never contemplated. Even if I could, I don't want to bear children just to fuck them up. I want to be a perfect woman, and a child always gets in the way.'

'We should talk about that…'

'We shouldn't. It's perfectly clear to me.'

My friend, I've had enough of this psychologist. Of him acting as though I can't make my way in life without him. Life works how people want it to work. Perhaps I was rather brusque with him, because after all he deserves my respect and gratitude; it was him who set this process in motion, organized everything, because I wouldn't have managed alone, I know. But just as I've cut the cord to the genital masculinity that was so oppressive, now I want to get away from all of this, tell everyone where to go, the doctors, my family, Raül, everyone and everything that formed part of what we might call my 'previous circumstance', my old life. It's not possible, I know, and the fact I can't get rid of the things that anger me like I got rid of that miserable dangle of flesh that so captivated mother makes me feel somehow defeated. When I show her my new female body, poor thing, she's definitely going to disown me and everything about my life.

My sister tells me to calm down, and reasons that if I've always felt like a woman, and can now feel complete, I can't feel more like a woman… But the leap to getting where I am has been so risky and so demanding.

I don't really understand why I should see the sexologist. So that he can brow-beat me again with his anachronistic morality? I should go though, if nothing else to show him what I've achieved through willpower and determination. Unless there are specific problems, I don't intend to see the neurologist or any of the others, because they didn't have much of a role when I was in hospital.

That's everything so far. I'll let you know how things go.

Be happy.
Ruth

Letter 17

My friend,

I went to see my parents with my sister. When I announced that I'd had surgery and that it had been successful, mother lost it completely.

'Poof, degenerate, traitor, invert…!'

I weather the outburst as best I can with my sister's help, unmoving at my side. When the initial onslaught is over, I suggest that she might like to see the results of my surgery. She lays into me, foul-mouthed:

'If you never had any balls to start with, what's there to be so smug about now?'

I roll up the skirt I'm wearing, take off my knickers and lie down on the sofa as if waiting for the gynaecologist.

'No! I don't want to see!' my mother screams.

But gradually she comes closer. I offer up my sex, now with a growth of soft pubic hair, to her eyes. Unable to resist, she looks and examines me.

'He's a girl!' she shouts, finally. 'The son of a bitch is a girl!' And she says to father, 'Look, look, we've got another girl! It's like she's just been born!' And then, in hysterics, her face contorted, she makes strange, incomprehensible sounds, although now and again a word comes through clearly. 'You back-stabbing bastard…' She spits at me. 'You will always be Raül, the male Raül…'

She starts shrieking and stamping her feet on the floor with increasing ferocity until Dad squares up and slaps her twice. She stops dead and drops into a chair, crying. Now dressed again, I go up to her, take her hand in mine and say, 'It's done, and there's no going back…'

'I wanted a boy,' she murmurs weakly. 'I had a boy, I wanted a man…, women are chaff, just an instrument for men, a refuge for their lust, the exile of the human condition. And what is your name, daughter?'

'Ruth.'

'It's a pretty name. You're pretty too… you look like me when I was younger.' She turns to father. 'Pass me our wedding photo.' She takes it in both hands and remarks, 'We're the same… Perhaps you are a woman.'

Her breathing quickens and the little pulsing vein at her temple seems more and more angry. She sits staring at me, almost motionless, and when she speaks, she seems delirious.

'The birth went well, but the labour was long. I didn't want the pregnancy; I'd already had one child. I didn't give birth to you, women like you give birth to themselves, they don't have a mother, just a path they follow as shadows, as objects which have never existed, phantoms of aborted desire, the scattered biography of horizons that is lost like waterless rain over the death of the sexes… there's no mother, you have no mother, no-one can know you… I want a son who can heal the wound, the ivory scar that you opened with spurts of blood, with sobs of penitence, murderous remembrance… there is no longer any sea of salvation, nor any stone on which to deposit the bones which have been the insignia of fermentations… we will never again see each other at the orbital crossroads, caught in an eternal trap… I will go away, far from where I've always been, while you will remain here subject to the destiny of amnesia…'

I am fascinated by her delirium, by its free association of unthought words, like surrealist writing or talking therapy on the psychoanalyst's couch. It is almost like a sentence of eviction declaimed from the throne of autonomous, unbridled words, the resonance of words that come from goodness knows where. Perhaps from the drug-like pain that numbs discernment and then lays waste.

Mother's words are the most striking she has pronounced in the whole of our personal history. I wonder why people don't use drugs more (alcohol or pain) and unleash our unconscious mind. Maybe we'd get along better, clash less with the armour of reason, and communication would be structured like a maternal fluid that still seeps through the umbilical cord…

My friend, please forgive my speaking so openly about the impact the visit to my mother has had on me, and especially her savage words. My sister hasn't taken much of this in beyond a general impression. She was there in the same way a passenger waiting for a train at the wrong station is there. I realised this as we were on our way back home and she was smiling unconcerned and I was almost in tears. Father was calm throughout, kissed me goodbye and said, 'you know where I am.'

I want to see Raül.

Be well.
Ruth

Letter 18

Dearest friend,

I almost don't go. I try to talk myself out of it a couple of times. The discussion I'd had with the sculptor before suggested we were polarized in terms of my genitality, and I've been thinking obsessively about what might happen if I go back again. In the end I take a deep breath, as though about to plunge into stormy seas, and knock.

'Hello, it's me,' I say, as he opens the door. He studies me carefully, surprised, before giving me a big hug.

'I wondered what on earth had happened to you.'

The reproach buffers him from my presence, which he must have been expecting. He steps back to admire me.

'You look stunning!'

I smile nervously.

'And so elegant.'

He embraces me again. Suddenly the first words he ever said to me spring back into my head: you're perfect, a perfect ephebe, celestial breasts and a little dick that holds the promise of every dick in the world. That's just how forms should be: suggested, insinuated, hinted at, barely evident. Always cherish this perfection because it's a gift from the gods, and you are the daughter of gods, not of men.

Those words echo in my mind, just as they did on the hospital trolley when I was coming round from the anaesthetic. Now I feel blocked, and he realises.

'You're so lovely,' he quips, 'shall we have some fun?!' before changing tack. 'So, ready to work?'

I don't answer because I've just caught sight of a what looks like a sculpture covered with a damp sheet in one corner of the studio. He follows my gaze.

'Do you want to see it?'

He removes the sheet.

'I've kept the clay damp because I want to make a few modifications. If you take off your clothes, I could do it now.'

His tone is professional, cool. He moves the piece to where the light is better and encourages me over to the familiar pedestal. I undress. He looks me up and down as if checking for the aspects he wants to retouch. Suddenly he stops still with his eyes fixed on my pubis. There's complete silence for a couple of seconds which seem to last an eternity. Then the silence is shattered.

'Noooooooooooooo!!' reverberates around the studio like the thunderous cry of a mountain giving birth.

'No! No! No!' He rubs his eyes with the heel of his hands and looks again, this time with curiosity. 'What have you done? Who's responsible for this sacrilege? The daughter of the gods has profaned the sanctuary of her perfection, the daughter of paradise has sinned and deserted her beauty…' He is quiet briefly and then shouts, 'This is an outrage!' He falls to his knees and starts weeping. 'Now you're just a common girl like all the girls in this ugly world. You've betrayed me, you've broken your word… the isles of fortuity no longer navigate your skin, the landscape of your body has lost the silence of timelessness and now recites futility in gulps.'

Words keep coming from his mouth as he approaches the sculpture. He stops within touching distance and sets to work feverishly. As he turns his back, I put my clothes on and head towards the door. Before I get there he walks up and grabs my arm roughly.

'I don't need you anymore,' he says. 'The divinity that you once were will be immortalised for eternity in the bronze this will become.' And then half-hissing, half-shouting, he commands, 'Get out!'

This is a lesson, in spite of its violence: art is an act of love. This I learn when I see that I've destroyed the artist's love object, when I witness the strength of his reaction, his grief. He tries to find some consolation in the permanence of my former likeness. As I leave I'm convinced that I'll never set foot in his studio again. But when I'm a sculptor, perhaps I won't be so far away. Will I be capable of such uncompromising devotion to my art?

When I've recovered my composure, I reflect that art, love, becomes a system of purification, a universal rhythm of which artists are the trustees. The individual has to die in order for their work to be born, and the work has to endure over time in order for the individual to exist. While I got dressed back at the studio, I was thinking that the sculpture of me would represent the demise of a not-wanting-to-be-what-one-isn't, the calque of a circumstance. By contrast, the work I create will have its roots in my resurrection, its power will be challenge, and the more real everyday life is, the more fictitious my work will be. This is where my creative oeuvre begins: I've made my body in the shape of my desire. I've made concrete the image that I have thought, wanted, demanded, contrary to nature's ambition for me. The journey has begun.

I'm not sure whether I've said everything I wanted to say, but you'll be able to make out the unwritten calligraphy between the lines.

Be well.
Ruth

Letter 19

My dear friend,

I've received a letter from a friend who did Fine Arts with me inviting our year group to a meal. I'm initially in two minds, so I consult my sister. She tells me I should go, because what I need now is contact with people my own age, because that will 'normalize' me.

Almost everyone is at the dinner, or at least those of us who graduated together. Luckily, I am sat next to the smart, friendly girls, and they are very kind to me. The dinner is a pretext for organising our degree celebration trip and, after throwing some ideas around, we decide on Greece, as a way of celebrating our status as future art professionals, whether as creatives or teachers.

After dinner we stay around chatting and soon form different groups, each according to affinity. My neighbour from the meal stays with me, and when we're alone she asks me round to her place for a drink. I accept. She lives uptown, in a big house she's inherited from her parents who died in a road accident. The house has a huge ground floor with a sizeable garden and swimming pool, cypresses and other trees and shrubs. She's relaxed as she shows me around, appreciative of her surroundings but also, I think, a little sad. We walk with glasses of red wine in our hands. At the other end of the pool there's a statue, a female, a life-sized nude.

'It's my mother. I sculpted her a couple of years ago…'

Then from one room to another, and finally to an annex.

'This is my workshop. It was my father's twenty-second birthday present to me.'

It's very spacious and well-illuminated. Everywhere there is work in progress or work in an apparently finished state.

'This year I'm thinking of exhibiting some pieces, even though it's a bit premature, but I've got to start somewhere and I've decided to go for it.' We leave our glasses on a shelf and she takes my hand and shows me around the studio. Then we go outside. 'This is where I work with bronze. This is the kiln for my clay and ceramics…'

We go back into the studio and she shows me the tools she uses to work clay, shape wood and carve marble... I'm fascinated.

'And where's your studio or workshop?' she asks, smiling.

I confess that I don't have one yet, not even close. She squeezes my hand hard as if to apologise for making me feel awkward. I squeeze her hand in turn.

'At the moment my work is figurative,' she explains, 'and the exhibition will demonstrate my talent for studies and sketches, and my dexterity with materials. I've got bigger plans for the future, riskier but more satisfying.'

Still holding my hand, she looks at me very deliberately and asks me what projects I have. I admit that everything's rather confused at present, and that I need time to get my life back on track. She doesn't seem to understand but is clearly curious. We go over to a bench and sit down. Leaning up against me, she puts an arm around my shoulder, and gently draws me close.

'Can I help?'

She brushes her thumb lightly over my lips, barely making contact. I let her. She moves her face close to mine and I feel the breath of a girl who's brimming with life. She kisses me. I enjoy the pressure of her mouth on mine, the moist warmth of her tongue as it slips between my lips and then probes deeper. After a few seconds she pulls back, smiles, and takes my face in her hands.

'You're lovely, Ruth...'

She unbuttons my blouse and checking my reaction, caresses my breasts.

'I'm not wearing a bra either.'

She takes off her own shirt and it's true. Her breasts are small but perfectly formed. She grasps my hand and invites me to touch her. I don't quite resist, but she has to take the lead. My palm feels her breast as a part of me. She cups mine in her hand and we kiss again. Almost without realising, we're naked but for our underwear. There's lust in her eyes as she runs her hands and lips over my body.

'You're magnificent, divine! Touch me, kiss me!'

I do so, receiving her body as a message full of mystery and desire. She kicks off her knickers and takes off mine. She kisses my abdomen and pubis, and just before she gets to my sex she's quiet.

'What a delicious vagina!' And she kisses me, sucking gently. As though indulging in some ancestral rite she puts her tongue inside me, and then throws herself onto the sofa, opens her legs, and offers herself to me.

'Put your mouth on me, I want you.'

She guides my head down towards her, and I do to her what she has done to me. She becomes more and more aroused until she comes hard in spasms that shake her over and over.

'More, don't stop…'

She positions me on the sofa so that her mouth is by my sex and mine is next to hers. The game that follows makes my head dizzy as her tongue penetrates my cunt, my arousal builds, my clitoris seems determined to ace its first night. We cry out together and our bodies convulse, entwined, and as we continue to kiss, so the spasms keep coming. Until we're done and melt into an exhausted embrace. After a long silence she whispers, 'I love you, I love you…'

Is it her who says that, or is it me? We're so into each other, our identification and surrender so complete, that it's difficult to tell where the voice comes from. My friend extricates herself and, still naked, gets up to pour two more glasses of wine, handing me one.

'I don't know what god sent you but here's to him…'

I watch her closely and wonder whether this girl isn't me, emerging from myself at my journey's end. We toast, set down the glasses on a side table, and she comes up to me again. When she's before me I kiss the top of her thighs as if I'm kissing mine and lick her sex as if I'm licking mine. I look at her and recognize myself in her body and give myself to her so she can do as she pleases. As she takes me in her arms and fucks me, I experience pleasure, so much pleasure. The neophyte voice in my head yells 'My sex works!'

My friend, when I get home, I think a lot about this encounter. I'd never given myself carnally to a woman with such abandon. Never had a woman kiss me on the mouth, perhaps because I'd never thought it possible. I'd never considered it at all because it simply wasn't on my horizon. As you know, my wish is to be a normal woman... but is it normal to be with a woman and experience sexual plenitude?

All of a sudden I'm struck by a new uncertainty: how do these orgasms with a female partner relate to those I first experienced? More specifically: are my latest orgasms the same as the others, of the same nature? Were the earlier orgasms hysterical ideations, as my psychoanalyst would say, and those just now the fruit of a normal nature functioning normally? Between our bodies, between my friend's orgasms and my own, there is no difference, because our convulsions flow from the same sensibility, the same result. It would seem, therefore, that I can celebrate coming of age – coming of nature – as a woman. One doubt remains, however: is it enough, or appropriate, that this proof should come from an encounter with another woman, or will I not be fully a woman unless I'm penetrated by a man?

My dear friend, perhaps my celebrations are a little premature.

Take care.
Ruth

Letter 20

My friend,

In one of my letters I explained that I want to be an intelligent woman with an attractive body, and capable of falling in love… with a man. I said that before a number of other things happened. Am I brave enough to say the same now? One of my girlfriends from Fine Arts and I have said we love each other. Perhaps it was said in the heat of that crazy tryst, in the midst of that delirium, that erasure of reality, that plunge into the abstraction of jouissance, into a state of utter purity. We confessed as much to each other, acknowledging the fevered nature of our declarations. The words were words, and their circumstance doesn't strip them of their reality. The certainty they expressed still echoes in my mind, or rather, in my sex. But while my sex was new, my brain had been working, thinking, trying to figure things out for a long time, learning what was possible, what wasn't, what would be best for me. What I wanted was one thing; the accidents of fate that shaped it were quite another. I wanted to be a woman and I've had the surgery, but where is my woman's sex taking me?

At the moment I'm surprised by these moments of happiness my girlfriend is creating, happiness I didn't look for or even imagine. My friend, I wish my head would be quiet, I wish it would stop analysing every thought, interrogating me. I want to be able to do what I want, to give in to my intuitions. In a way that's what happened with my girlfriend because my judgement had no part in that erotic game at all; we were just transported by an overwhelming impulse. I get a lot of satisfaction from that experience, even though it was not what I'd planned: that is, to derive pleasure from being penetrated by a man, from having a penis in my vagina, rubbing against my clitoris.

Why do you think I'm so stubborn? Why do I insist on conforming to a single model of identification so blindly, the most commonplace model, the model most widely accepted by the majority of society? After all, that's why I had surgery. If I'd wanted to be unique, I could have stayed as I was, as I came into the world. Now I've had surgery,

I've fallen into the trap of becoming socialised according to this particular model, and every alternative is viewed with suspicion. I pose myself the problem, and I resolve it. That's how it is, because no-one else can help me, because no-one can join me in my solitude. We try to be accepted by the majority as though we're a political party looking to win elections in a democratic state, when victory isn't to be found with the majority but in the successive pacts that the person makes with him or herself. My pact was to choose to be a woman. But I don't know what kind of woman. What does the female condition depend on? Only on having an attractive vulva? I can have no complaints on that score anyway. What's disconcerting is that the appreciation of my genitals has come from another woman.

My friend, I'm sorry to keep repeating myself, but you know that you help me find my way along this path with its uncertain horizon. One day this week I'd like to get together with Raül, at home, just to make love. I'll let you know how it goes.

Be well.
Ruth

My friend,

I went shopping for clothes before I met up with Raül. Although it hadn't been my intention, I quite compulsively bought several frivolous items of lingerie. Why? Do I need to seduce him? Without even articulating it as such, I'd fallen for a cliché, for a mechanism by which women tempt men into sex. Yet I don't need to use bribery to get what I want.

You know I have to analyse everything, especially the motivation underlying my improvised behaviour, and perhaps I should acknowledge that quite unintentionally I've let myself be taken in by the fantasy of wanting to be more woman for Raül and, if I'm honest, more sexy. And we're back to the same question: don't I feel myself to be a woman, enough of a woman, already? Before surgery I was absolutely clear that I wanted to be what I wasn't, and now that genitally I am who I want to be, is it enough to want? I'm sorry to admit that, as a woman, I'm behaving like a woman who has superficial values that don't sit comfortably with me. Or could it be the case, as I've said before, that I'm still not woman enough, and therefore haven't yet attained that headspace, those behaviours or resources that women enjoy? Where and what is the crux of the female condition? Am I led by reductive thinking which means that I can only entertain either/ or, and not both/and? This would be the before and after of surgery, for example, as if qualifying as a woman were determined by this alone. Are women born, or are they made in the process of living as women? As you know, I wasn't born a woman, but I am a woman because I accept femaleness as the single most significant protagonist in my life; it is what makes me more myself every day. And what is 'myself' in my case?

Even as I'm writing to you, words whose meanings are alien to me fill my head: I water the triangle of memory with the moisture of desire, with my back turned on affection I build cathedrals which become beach sand, without my body I head for the irrigation channels of invisible roses, I hope to be the triumphant resident of all absences, I will be unrepeatable when eternity kisses my aura… Messages that seemed to come from deep within or far beyond.

I put on my new lingerie in front of the mirror and am happy with my body, this inescapable dwelling of pleasure, or perhaps death. The underwear seems to magnify me, and my body alone attracts me. I'm aware of what I'm saying: I feel myself attracted to my body, I am the object of my female body's attraction. I stroke my body over and underneath my lingerie. The palms of my hands brush my skin like warships tasting moss, a voluminous craving, the fevered extremes of silence, the submission of every nook and cranny read by my finger-tips… and I caress my sex. My female sex! As though I am a newborn in front of the mirror. And without any convulsion or spasm that might drag me from reality, I feel full of me, reassured by the union of hands and body, a body of epithelial pleasure. And I stand there, breathing steadily, my breasts fuller as though suddenly coming into their own: my lips teasing my nipples through the mirror. My body possessed and enjoyed by that same body deep within the labyrinthine pathways towards a landscape of light… or darkness. The whole of me a geography illuminated by darkness, by a past without memory, a history exsanguinated. My warship has come through the storm without a coffin. I am in the beam of the lighthouse.

And I still have time to take a walk and enjoy the city, an anony-mous proclamation of my discovery. This evening I'm meeting Raül. I'll tell you about it next time. Forgive me for these long, rambling paragraphs; I don't know where they've come from.

Be well.
Ruth

My dear friend,

Raül and I meet in a bar close to where I live. Immediately he sets eyes on me and says I look fabulous. I fill him in on everything that has happened since we've last seen each other. Very little of what I say seems new to him.

'You look good too.'

We have a few drinks and then walk for a while to take some pressure off the occasion. He knows perfectly well what is on my mind, but I don't know what will happen. He talks to me about the film *Life is Beautiful*, which he'd viewed very differently from many people, and the critics in particular.

'It's shamelessly pro-USA and the final scenes don't make sense in the context of a script that seems to want to be a hymn to life and yet ends in an easy surrender to death.'

I like hearing Raül's opinions. He says he's also read several collections of poetry and recites some lines to me.

'That's real poetry, not like the postcard or telegram messages some people compose.'

He comes up with a few examples from memory and we both laugh.

We're home before we realise. I offer him a glass of red wine because I know it's his favourite late-night drink. When we're sitting on the sofa he brings up the subject of my surgery.

'How do you feel?'

'Really good, so good that I'd like us to make love...'

Raül seems to understand these words as a nervous exaggeration on my part. I take my clothes off till I'm in my underwear, slip off my shoes, and stand in front of him. He looks at me approvingly. He holds out his arms, draws me into him and kisses me, stroking my neck and back. He removes my remaining clothing and lays me down on the sofa.

'You're perfect...'

He quickly undresses, comes close and examines my pubis.

'What a masterpiece.'

He caresses me until he's hard and I notice his penis seems bigger and thicker than ever. I'm afraid. He lifts me up from the sofa and kisses me, and I feel his penis between my thighs. He covers me with kisses and moistens my vulva with his tongue. He goes to do the same to my anus but stops even before I've had time to react because he knows that I'm not into that. He kisses my breasts softly.

'Are you ready for me to push into you?'

He sounds like he's talking about a laboratory experiment and I have the sense his erection's still growing. I lie down on the sofa again and open my legs. I'm dry, but he's ready with lube. He starts to penetrate me, gradually, as though he's taking my virginity. And that's what's happening, in effect. Little by little, his whole sex is inside me. My premiere. I feel invaded. I feel as though a strange body is inside me, as though I am profaned, adulterated. Why do I have the image of my father in my head, what's he doing in this scene? And what does mother think she's missing out on in this secret intimacy? Maybe they're fighting, maybe she wants to rescue her man, who is now just Raül. She wants to be inside him, take the lead. The image blurs and they disappear.

Raül moves rhythmically, respectfully, like a piston, as though my femaleness were also a very delicate piece of lab equipment. He buries himself deep inside me. One moment like a fireball that violates the midwives, like a wind that takes hold of the crystal of silences, and the next like a hoof that sharpens sacred epithelia. I can't bear to be penetrated a moment longer and I shove Raül hard to get him out of me. He withdraws in practised fashion and seems to take it in his stride. We end up like two strangers in a hospital waiting room. He refills his glass and mechanically drinks a couple of mouthfuls. I don't know where I am. I can't grasp this bitter rupture in the fabric of destiny.

After a few minutes, Raül attempts to break my trance, asking me if I want to try again.

'Noooooo!'

I'd screamed out wildly, as if all the seaweed in all the seas were dragging me under. I cry, sensing an unusual moisture. Droplets of blood. Raül tries to console me, still erect. But I can't stand his words or his hands, and I shrink back.

'Leave me alone, please…'

He dresses and I thank him before he leaves.

'You'll always be a good friend.'

Still naked, I look to see where the blood is coming from. It's a tiny amount, but enough to stain two fingers. I look at it as though it's a flag proclaiming my womanhood, but a flag at half-mast. The penetration was an insult. My body has lost something of its essence, defeated but defiant.

A month later I ask Raül if we can try again, and he agrees. I quickly realise that it isn't going to work: I can't bear having a man inside of me.

I'm desperate to get together with my sculptor girlfriend but she's out of town. I cry.

That's all for now.

Be well.
Ruth

Letter 23

My friend,

I've struggled to process my experience with Raül and arranged to see the psychoanalyst. I explain the first and second encounters in detail, holding nothing back. At the end, distressed by the effort of recollection, I raise my voice.

'I don't want a penis in my life. I gave up my own, and now I renounce every penis in the world. The male sceptre has no place inside me, no intruder gets to violate my female diadems. I've surrendered what I wasn't in order to be a woman, cut off my dick. Through this act I've emasculated every man in the world, every single one. I want to know nothing of men, because they've ceased to exist, and they can't be my complement. Raül will still be a close friend, but he'll never again be my lover. I'm a self-sufficient woman, I don't need a man to be happy... The friend from my course, the sculptor, is more than enough, the love of woman to woman, symmetrical love, mirror to mirror, no penetration to alter the clandestine equilibria, just hands that carry away the secrets of my skin like a flock of birds.'

When I say this, the psychoanalyst asks me to tell him about this relationship and I do so willingly, graphically even, with words like blinding sparks.

'I'm in love with her because she brings me cloistered silence, flesh memento, frontiers sliced in two, sacramental skin that yearns for the baptismal pasture of saliva and a strong, ploughing tongue... I am in love, I am a lion rampant in the soaring spires of this tender text, and I hear the late hours chime out a purifying fire, one body moulded by another, the celebration of unified substance... I love this woman, and this love makes me feel the best woman. At her side the walls of the labyrinth crumble and there emerges a metropolis of fidelity.'

He lets me say everything I want to say, exactly as I dare say it. It's a long while before he speaks. He talks about the Oedipus complex, penis envy, the phallic mother, childhood fixation on the father's penis, phantasm...

'Rubbish, utter rubbish!'

It's an exclamation of rejection, a rebellion against this enlightened professional speculation. I take a deep breath and then thank him for everything he's done to progress my case, and I do so sincerely, noting that without him, none of this would have been possible. When he sees that I've cooled down, he brings up the subject of female homosexuality, describing it as an uncomplicated and fulfilling outcome, the result of freedom of choice, an unintended, unimagined resolution. Before I leave, he asks me what my career plans are.

'I want to be a sculptor.'

'You don't want to write?' he chuckles. When we talk, some of the things you say are wonderfully poetic. Catalan literature is in a dreadful state... But poetry could help you articulate the anxiety that you're almost certainly going to experience at some point.'

Perhaps it's true that I've been more forthright than usual in some of the things I've said. I'll have to talk to Raül. Then we say goodbye like two old friends.

I walk as though reborn: I feel brand new. I hear questions form inside my head from somewhere deep within: have I made the right choice? Do I know what I'm experiencing? I've insisted so often on the here and now, have I actually arrived anywhere? What don't I know about life yet? What measure of who I am awaits me...?

Some of the men who walk close by cast glances in my direction, as if they hear the words that my silence speaks.

Nothing else. Take care.
Ruth

Letter 24

My dear friend,

 I think we can say that there's a certain stability to my life at the moment. My girlfriend the sculptor and I are very much in love, and we tell each other so, especially when we make love, often and passionately. I find it so easy to give myself to her, hold nothing back, so much so that if initially I'd considered any kind of anal eroticism as taboo, one day it was actually me who shamelessly initiated anal play. First I'd gazed on her backside as a vision never before seen, as though a landscape of throbbing apses had appeared before me. Then I worked my tongue into her anus. She reciprocated, with even more enthusiasm. I didn't expect it to be so sexually sensitive, even orgasmic. The warmth of our lips and the moist steel of our tongues became tools of pleasure. It wasn't lost on me that she'd performed a kind of penetration, that she'd entered me. And it made me happy. Almost as though she were me. But she was her. When she was inside me I urged her over and over to keep going, and begged her to let me penetrate her again. We lay there for what seemed ages, my head by her feet and vice-versa, while a series of spasms still shook both of us. Mouth, lips, tongue inside, as if the gates of a spectacular fortress had just opened.

 At the beginning we made love every time we saw each other like addicts. Then one day we agreed that we needed to refocus, find some self-discipline, and from that day onwards, we worked seriously.

 She gave me the freedom of her workshop. At first I was a little lost, because although I'd learned the techniques as part of my Fine Arts degree, I was surrounded by such an embarrassment of materials, I didn't know where to start. And then, from nowhere, I picked up a length of stainless steel, about fifteen centimetres square and slightly more than a metre long, and I wrapped some hessian fabric around the middle, like a scarf a couple of palms wide. It looked good, but the hessian wouldn't stay in place. I applied a really strong varnish which fixed it firmly where I wanted it. My girlfriend and I looked at it, re-flected, analysed, and agreed that it could be improved. The idea was good but I needed to develop it further. For days I wandered around, picking up items, considering textures, and then suddenly it hit me.

'That's it! The hessian has to be made of bronze!'

My friend knew I had no experience of smelting metals, and she helped me through the process, step by step. We managed to cast the hessian in bronze and polish it, although retaining some of the greenish tonalities that contrasted pleasingly with the yellows of the polished sections. Finally, we mounted it on the steel column, like the original hessian scarf. We were both impressed, and we kissed.

'I think you've found a rich vein.'

This was the piece that made me a sculptor. Aware of my less fortunate circumstances, my friend let me have the materials free of charge.

'When you sell something, you can pay me back.'

That was what spurred us to exhibit our art together: hers figurative, mine abstract. But I really had to get down to work.

Be well.
Ruth

Letter 25

My friend,

I asked father if he'd transfer me some money so that I could pay for the materials I need and so that I could work without being financially reliant on my girlfriend, who's already letting me share her workshop and her life, in fact. Father was generous, as always.

If until recently my head couldn't stop thinking, I'm now over-come with emotions and besieged by a heightened state of sensation that occupies my every moment. My sculptor girlfriend is present in me twenty-four hours a day, and I feel her within me like a substance that fills all the space that my solitude once inhabited. Because I was so used to examining everything, I thought that sentiments and emotions could also be analysed. But it quickly dawned on me that they can't be externalised and subjected to calculation and suspicion. Every time I tell my friend that I love her, my breath quivers with the ineffable, with some entity that swerves the concreteness of words as though I had never been a part of them at all. Our lack of self-knowledge and our ignorance of who we are: this is the origin of love.

My friend, I wouldn't say that love is about conscious desire or will, not at all. It's the necessity of coming out of the darkness within, from where time is minimal and volition is null. Words alone are not up to the task of declaring love; they need creative calligraphy, artistic testimony, other voicings of the ineffable. Maybe the body becomes a barrier that prevents us, somehow, from attaining that ultimate destiny. Art fills us, nourishes us, like broth. Art walks in the footsteps left by desire and, as it makes its way, stokes the illusion of omnipotence necessary to discover the unknown. And all of this unsettles our being, our leaving and returning from where we are and have never been: endowed with dazzling brightness, a brilliance that blinds; glorifying in life, idolising the destination we did not choose in the dark. I adore my lover.

From this position of adoration, of reverence, I understand how beauty adorns our persons, hers and mine, and we identify in a single being. I understand that my lover and I are the beauty that transcends material, body-to-body reality, that attains higher planes of essence. After we make love, our bodies exhausted, this is when we are able to contemplate its pure sign, or sublime semiotics, as our aesthetics professor would say; a syntagm and its meaningful chain of signifiers: the work of art. Perhaps this is why we love each other so much: we are two values of beauty, beauty that we delight in through our love, and that love sublimates into perfect surrender when we are physically intimate. My lover and I, she and I, me written in her corporeal design and in the beauty that encapsulates everything about me, incommunicable fact, proof of the being transferred to the other and made thirsty by distance, by the non-existent grail. Only by ceasing to exist will we know the destination. After multiple orgasms I often taste perfection. Death is the conclusion of the quest, the perfection of triumph.

And why, my friend, am I talking about death when I'm radiant with life, with love, projects, and ever-increasing spaces in which to exhibit my hegemony? I have my rose; I have no use for its thorns.

Be well.
Ruth

Letter 26

My friend,

I'm so happy! So happy! Love, art, beauty… My partner and I are working hard. I'm basing my pieces on the steel I found, as well as aluminium and other metals, in combination with the bronze-cast hessian. I've already created ten variations on the theme. My girlfriend's also been prolific: busts (heads), breasts, backsides, all as stand-alones, and I'm sitting for her. She spends a lot of time sculpting me in clay, and when we want a break we lie on a kind of big bunk that we put together in the studio and covered with carpet. She doesn't miss a chance to caress me even though she already knows every inch of my body. Sometimes we end up kissing each other until we climax. Then we talk about our work, but never about our lives. This means that she doesn't know who I am or how I came to be a woman. I feel, I am, and that's enough. Both of us are interested in our life as it is right now.

One day we decide to clear our heads and have dinner in one of those restaurants with a dance floor. On a neighbouring table there are two middle-aged men who keep staring at us. They came over when they've finished eating.

'Would you like to join us for a drink?'

'We'd be delighted!' my friend says.

We sit down at their table and order champagne. After the second glass we get up to dance. The music is slow with an easy rhythm. The man I dance with first holds me gently around the waist, but little by little comes closer until his hips brush mine. Suddenly I feel his erection. Ew! I push him away and look around for my friend. She's dancing with the other man. I take hold of her arm and pull her towards another part of the room where we dance without inhibition.

'What a vile lech!'

'Mine too!'

As we dance, we pass in front of our two would-be suitors and wave at them, kissing each other full on the mouth, our bodies pressed tightly together.

Our show clearly isn't to their taste, and they make to reclaim us, as if we are their property. Such is their rudeness, my friend becomes really angry and with a well-coordinated elbow and knee leaves one of them writhing on the floor. The other stands motionless, eyes on the scene. Two bouncers arrive, alerted by the commotion, and without a single word being exchanged, accompany the men to settle their tab, and throw them out. Not before my girlfriend has gestured that they'll be paying for our meal too, and off we dance, and drink, until there isn't a drop of champagne left.

In our euphoric state, we order another bottle, and how we dance! Everyone is watching us, and at one moment, they burst into applause. Like a magnet we draw other couples onto the floor to dance, and to our surprise, they are all women. The men stay at their tables, nonplussed. The atmosphere is hot, wild, and we swap partners. I dance with all manner of good-looking women: blondes, brunettes and one whose skin is almost red. And we dance, and we drink. When the women see that my girlfriend and I kiss each other ferociously every time we coincide on the dance floor as a couple, they imitate us, and there comes a moment when the women stop dancing and start kissing each other as though nothing else matters in the world. And then without warning, one of the participants in the mayhem plants herself in the middle of the dance floor and strips down to her underwear. There are howls of protest from the other dancers because she hasn't removed all her clothing. She resists for a moment but then gives in to the wishes of her audience. As she takes off her knickers there are startled gasps: that shapely woman has a penis; from her navel down, she is male. I very nearly faint. When my girlfriend sees the colour drain from my face she quickly leads me away, and a waiter shows us into a side room. I lie down and begin to recover myself.

'Are you okay? I've never seen you so terrified.'

'Maybe I've had too much to drink... or I'm not used to dancing...'

When my colour returns, we leave. She comes home with me and doesn't move from my side until I've regained my good humour.

Initially I think I might spend the night at hers, but I can't muster up the courage. I am afraid that we'll talk and she'll find out the reason for my reaction, and that will change the nature of our relationship with consequences I can't begin to guess at. I need to downplay what's happened, tiptoe around it. I condemn it to oblivion, locked and bolted in a closet of human remains as though it has all been a dream.

The following day we meet up at her studio to work as though nothing untoward has happened. But my mind is in turmoil. Perhaps there'd been nothing there and it had all been an image conjured up in my head by tiredness and alcohol. It made me think about the way I'd been on display in front of my father and mother, the military panel, my friends, everyone who was in a position to testify to my historical reality as if my authenticity now were just a sham, as though there existed a residual me inside that was capable of superimposing itself on the real outside. How long before this hegemonic internal pulse disappears?

Am I marked by duality? Why has this referent that I thought dormant suddenly woken up again?

Nothing happens without a reason, my friend, and perhaps that's why I'm so given to overthinking things.

Be well.
Ruth

My dear friend,

Not a day goes by without our seeing each other and we work enthusiastically and with huge optimism. And we like the pieces we produce. My girlfriend with her figurative impressions of my fragmented body and, at the moment, specifically, my buttocks. She's created several and arranged them in a tower alternating with my pubis, six pieces in all. At the moment she's working in clay, and then she wants to cast in oxidised bronze. I'm fully occupied with a large-scale sculpture in high-strength aluminium: a thirty-by-thirty box section, two metres high. I wanted to put a sixty-degree twist in the middle to create a spiral, without sacrificing the edges of the ridges. I've created the original positive in cardboard, but I don't feel confident enough to transfer it to its definitive medium in this workshop. My partner recommends that I visit a metallurgical plant she knows, gives me the address, and off I go. The staff are incredibly helpful. They're going to put together some samples and then we'll make a decision.

Today my girlfriend wants to party, and we throw ourselves onto the studio bunk and make love energetically. She pays particular attention to my backside, as if wanting to check its volume, structure and rhythm, and we kiss ravenously, indiscriminately. But I realise I'm not getting aroused as I would normally, and I am a long way from climax. When she comes strongly, I don't feel I have any choice but to fake an orgasm, even exaggerate it. What's wrong with me? I'm pretty sure that the restaurant scene the other night, and its phantasm, are blocking me mentally. But I insist on continuing so she won't notice, and redouble my attentions, saliva, tongue, vagina, anus. She becomes aroused again and just when I think all is lost, I start to feel my orgasm build as she reciprocates, and we come together, gloriously. I scream out: 'I'm clean, clean!'

She doesn't respond and I feel liberated. The phantasm is dead and buried. Or do phantasms in fact die? One of my lectures in the Faculty of Fine Arts had been on art and psychoanalysis, and at some point the professor had said that the phantasm never dies, and if we think it's buried, it nevertheless comes back and it's this that contributes a specific dynamic to the work of art. Perhaps that's right, but I think we can get used to living with the phantasm and not be constantly reminded of its presence. Is that how we defeat its hegemony?

We've got enough pieces for an exhibition now!

Take care.
Ruth

Letter 28

My dear friend,

Please indulge me because I can't wait to try to explain this. Here goes: the unfathomable mystery of love precedes loving sentiment, as though the experience of love already exists in the mystery, but until love has been experienced, becomes experience, the mystery inhabits an existential void. I'd add that if there is no experience of love, love becomes something it is not, despite being what it is. I'll tell you what's filling my head and making me so happy because no-one else is going to hear this from me.

A person carries within them the substance of all the projects that may ever be possible but have not yet been realised. So love is one such project which will become emotion and deep affection. And there you have it! I'm in love, I know I'm in love, madly in love with my friend and, thanks to her, love has completely taken hold of me, even made me crazy, because it turns reality upside down and transforms it. Perhaps my inane chatter will have you think that I'm actually trying to invent love, or at least justify it, but no matter how many times I think this through I know that I love her because I feel this emotion, this ardour.

I'm finishing the aluminium column with the twist in the middle. I just need to wrap the two ends in bronze hessian. We have sufficient pieces to put on a really great exhibition, and we're ready to start looking for a gallery to host us. We'll show photos of our work to the gallery owners and, if we can, have them come to the studio. The first place I thought of was a gallery specialising in sculpture that had just opened, owned by a woman. There's no shortage of galleries, for sure, but very few dedicated to sculpture.

I met up with Raül. It was he in fact who was keen to find out how I was getting on. I talked to him about my work, and about being in love. When I confessed that the object of my affections was a woman, he seemed surprised. Up to a point, anyway. He knows me well and knows that my life takes unexpected turns. Even so, given how I'd reacted last time we were together, he could hardly be shocked by my new choice of partner. He offered me sage words.

'Take care with this kind of involvement, because your friend may feel more or less attracted to you, more or less curious about a lesbian relationship which might be short or last a long time, whereas your emotional attachment is likely to be more complex because your femininity originates in the rejection of your male nature rather than in the affirmation of a natural femaleness.'

I was furious. 'What the hell do you know about the intricacies of my existence!'

I was angry that he'd raised a subject I hadn't yet worked through, but which could actually be a possibility. I know that Raül is fond of me and what he says isn't a reproach but his way of helping me find lasting stability. But stability is what I already have! And I'll protect it tooth and nail. No-one gets to question my love... He didn't rise to my anger, though.

'Please, let me explain,' he said, calmly and gently. 'When you rejected your external male attributes, you rejected a virile condition and had a long process of transition in mind. But the male experience you've lived, willingly or otherwise, might still survive somewhere deep within the darkest recesses of your being, and it might appear at any time and steer your desire in other directions...'

'What are you blathering on about?' I said. 'My emotions, my will, the surgery and the hormone therapy – there's no way back.'

I was arguing, he was reflecting. I was the great protagonist of a process that in practice was over and done. But in fact, Raül's discomfort didn't arise from my actions, from my love for another woman, but rather from the possibility that this woman might one day not love me as she loves me now. And this possibility had never crossed my mind, and now the doubt is there and it bothers me.

'Never, she accepts me totally, and we make love as though time doesn't exist, without measure because we are the measure of all measures. I am in her and she is in me as a whole together, forever. You can't possibly understand!'

'The difference is that she has never been male, and you have…'

I don't want to see Raül ever again, and don't want him to put uncomfortable ideas in my head, make me insecure about where I am and what I have. And it hurts me to lose his friendship. I've had to give up so much and it won't be easy.

Take care.
Ruth

My friend,

We've given our exhibition pieces a trial run in the workshop, playing with different configurations. First we organised the work into two groups, one hers and one mine, with a gap in between. Initially it seemed to work until it occurred to me that we had worked together for so long, it didn't now make sense to separate our pieces when we should really be more together than ever. She completely agreed and we're trying to curate the show around a more unifying theme, alternating pieces by authorship. At the moment it's lacking harmony and seems quite muddled. It needs to be more coherent and we'll work on a different combination that'll be more pleasing to the eye. My girlfriend suggests that the gallery itself might prefer a different order.

'Let's leave things how they are for now and see if we can get a gallery owner to come and have a look.'

There are sixty-six pieces in total, and we spend a long time examining them from different angles. They all look good. We hug each other and kiss in celebration.

'Do you love me?' I ask.

She looks at me quizzically and gives me a lingering kiss. I insist. 'Will you always love me, always?'

She detaches herself from me, half-amused and half-enigmatic.

'Time doesn't exist, my dear, only the present; and the present is what counts, the state of now which succeeds itself but never generates a future…' She is more serious now. 'We have to take advantage of the present, live it intensely without trying to figure out its past, where it's come from; the past only exists as a collection of useless residues.' She then gazes into my eyes and kisses me hard, saying, 'Let's make love as a mark of what we've created.'

But she doesn't take the initiative and I'm disappointed. She kisses me passionately again and pauses as she invites my tongue to engage with hers. I accept and, conjoined in this way, we look over each piece in turn as if wanting to remind ourselves of their origin, that's to say, deep down inside ourselves where each was born as a projection of our desire. Finally we fall on to the bunk and in a state of high arousal she presses me down, removing my clothes. Little of what I say is intelligible, except, perhaps, the following.

'It's easy to undress a body; it's much more difficult to undress the soul...'

Maybe she doesn't want to hear what I say because she's so consumed in the passion of the moment. We make love till we come with an orgasm I want more than ever and which almost takes my head off. But straightaway I feel strangely sad.

We just have to get a gallery on board.

Be well.
Ruth

My friend,

We've taken dozens of photos, chosen the best ones and compiled a portfolio that shows our work to its best advantage. It's a really attractive brochure.

The female gallery owner who only deals in sculpture is very welcoming. She's quite young, perhaps thirty-five, with blonde, slightly curly hair. She dresses with a casual elegance, and is attractive and physically well-proportioned. Her eyes seem to draw us in. She explains that she enjoys discovering new styles, people who may be under the radar.

'Most galleries work with established artists, or those who are more or less accepted. But that's no fun, and there's no risk attached. The mafias who control the market like it that way. The art market is brutal; it's so degraded that it's essentially a brand business now. What matters is the signature of the author; we might as well be selling kitchen appliances. I'm interested in novelty, in what's really new. I like being challenged by art's ability to surprise.' While she talks, her eyes remain fixed on us. 'You're right to present your work as a single collection. And if I may, I'm not sure what I find more disconcerting, your breasts and backsides, or your abstractions. But I need to see everything for myself.'

She comes to the workshop and we receive her without ceremony, as if she's a regular visitor. She gets down to work immediately, taking in the whole collection first, and then surveying each piece in turn. When she finishes her first circuit, she starts again.

'Very good, let's do this. We need to get a catalogue together. I'll send a photographer.' She indicates three of my works, and three of my girlfriend's. 'I'll write the text and arrange the layout.'

We go into the other room and sit on the sofa. My girlfriend pours us each a glass of red wine which we savour approvingly, and toast to the success of the exhibition.

'I don't know what kind of reception you'll get, but I can

guarantee that everyone who's anyone will hear about it. I'll line up the critics.' Changing tack, she asks if we're married, separated. We say neither, because we're young and free. Then she launches into a little speech. 'The male-female couple is a problem because the man will never understand the woman, it's that simple. I was in a relationship for three years and the sex was good, but one day I realised that male eroticism is a world away from a woman's, at least in my case. When we were in bed, my partner was more and more absent, or perhaps it was me who felt more alienated in the relationship.'

We said nothing. 'You two look as though you've got a really great mutual understanding, as artists and as friends.' Then point-blank she asks, 'Do you make love?'

My girlfriend and I look at each other, startled. Neither of us knows what to say, and I even feel violated. What does this woman want? Our silence gives us away.

'I'm sorry, I got carried away by my own situation. I'll be honest with you: my crisis kicked off when I met a woman…'

The gallery owner is still drinking and her hand gestures are more expressive, asserting her presence as a woman who should be of interest to us. She wants to lure us in, seduce us even. Her skirt rides up to the top of her thighs. She's dark and her skin is finely textured. My head's spinning and I don't know what's happening. My girlfriend moves closer to her and looks at her as though they've known each other a lifetime. They share a smile. Suddenly they've cut the preliminaries and are kissing. I'm perplexed and their hands are all over each other. I don't believe what I'm seeing. My girlfriend edges the woman's skirt to the top of her thighs and gasps with surprise.

'I never wear knickers,' mentions the gallery owner, nonchalantly.

She pulls her skirt up around her waist, and I recognize the beauty of what's before me. My friend fondles her, undressing, and then buries her head between the woman's legs. The gallery owner beckons me over in her heightened state, and I move as though pulled on a string, fascinated. She asks me if she can kiss my sex, and I'm still so astonished that I feel unable to react. She lies on the sofa and I straddle her face. I'm tense, in the grip of an inescapable force. They gasp and explode in loud convulsions. I'm not aroused at all but I don't want to spoil their party and fake my own orgasm. That's not the end of it though, and the others seem to want to ride every last wave. I'm really ill at ease and leap off the sofa. Is this the cost of our exhibition? I feel deep shame and bitter frustration. I thought my friend made love with me because she loved me. Is it possible to make love without love? But I also feel ridiculous and naïve for not accepting this price. They've always been women, their sexuality has always been the way it is and the way they want it to be. Otherwise, why would two women who don't know each other behave in this way? I remember the first time I felt her skin on mine. My friend and I didn't know each other either. So why am I struggling to get my head around their intimacy? Will they fall in love? Will I be ignored? Love seems to be such a chaos of unpredictable effects.

My friend, when will I stop doubting and feeling so insecure?

Take care.
Ruth

My dear friend,

I feel awkward, inept. How long will I be tied to situations in which the body is lord and master? Sometimes I wonder what this tyranny is, this oppression that has everything depend on the friction between two bodies and their orgasms. Aren't orgasms just a form of plaint entombed by the hegemonic weight of flesh, or sobs that carry the soul's gasps? I don't know how much my desire is simply eagerness to finally be what I am still not completely, a process of becoming, or just striving, that causes me so much suffering. I would love to know when a person is herself completely, and when she has become a collage of borrowings from others.

I feel very alone and I have no-one else to talk things over with. Words, my friend! This is letter number thirty-one and perhaps they're all vestiges of what I've experienced, my life as a kind of eviction that inflicts wounds that sometimes cleave my identity and open my flesh. My girlfriend is wrong when she says that time past doesn't exist. I used to think that I should be able to erase this past, but every single day I've felt the weight of its gravity like a mass that still shapes me as it lays siege from every angle of adversity. All lives are marked or conditioned by the past and there's nothing we can do to prevent it. Breaking away or smashing it into fragments of unremembering, piling sediment on top as we go on living and burying it in the silt of our personal history, this would be tantamount to mutilating ourselves as a unity that embraces each and every day we live and have ever lived. It's impossible to maintain the illusion that we are new at each moment without being aware of the body that consumes itself in constant repetition and with each iteration generates death in order to be reborn from itself. How I'd love not to have a past, not to have any memory of what preceded me and believe that I've always been the girl I am now!

What do I need in order to know who I am? What are my weapons and my battlefield? Or can I only exist in the indifference of disorder and confusion? People are who they want to be, and so I'm not going to lazily blame destiny. But there is a kind of force that shifts us within the realm of chance and necessity, the force of improvisation and rule that we cannot escape. I feel naked and defeated in the presence of this force as if my will and determination are futile. Have I committed the error of wanting to subjugate this force and lead it towards horizons indicated by the example of others? My friend, which body is mine, the one I had before or the one I have now? Which is more authentic? Where does the certification of my birth end? And the certification of my transition? It's nonsensical for me to be asking these questions now, but I can't help myself. I suspect that no matter how many female signifiers I acquire, there'll always be an element of confusion. Perhaps my cells carry some kind of genetic freight that pushes my brain in one direction, my heart in another and my desire somewhere else: the dregs of my chaotic conception.

These are my thoughts in darkness, where clarity shines brightest. When I've explored them, I pass them on to you in written form, which is a way of working through them again. In the end, as I said before, perhaps everything is just residue, the ashes that a persistent beat keeps warm. And now I'll say something you won't expect to hear: I know that my nature then, and now, is different, and I accept this difference. Without it, these letters would never have been written, and I might never have been aware of it. Why do we assume unthinkingly that the majority share a common experience, when we don't know anything about their lives? While other people might take off their clothes to become naked and offer their body, I'd like to rip off my skin to offer my soul, get rid of my body to lay bare the real me. Maybe this would be the real act of love: know who we are, love ourselves from within, plant the flag of purity. The idea transcended by itself, without any material limitation; a speck of light that contains all possible beauty, kindness, happiness... More words! If I wrote to you about trivial things, perhaps I'd come across as more feminine, closer. If the feminists could hear me, they'd say I was male on the basis of those words alone!

My letters are an index of tortuous inquiry, an exercise in time-wasting, if not a text in which I lose and then re-find myself, over and over. Alone, or accompanied by myself? I would love to know about musical composition, because every letter would be a collection of notes that'd help you to understand what I say, everything that escapes rational conceptualisation. I am rational, as you've seen, but very often the primary substance of our whole raison d'être slips away from me.

I'm done for now, although I'd like to continue. Before I end, I want to say that sometimes I feel as though I'm part of a theatrical performance in which everyone tries to forget their role. Perhaps that's why I'm so fond of music, because it's an abstract medium in which I feel at home.

Be well.
Ruth

Letter 32

My friend,

I arranged to meet up with Raül again. I know you'll be surprised, but I really needed to talk. He agreed and we arranged to see each other at his house, because there's no-one around. I know the last time we were together I said I never wanted to see him again, never wanted anything to do with another man. So why have I gone back to him? Very simply, to take revenge on my sculptor girlfriend for her infidelity with the gallery owner. It's that basic, primal. Raül very tactfully asks how I'm getting on, and I fill him in on a few anodyne details. It's evening, and he opens a couple of beers. As we sit there on the sofa, I feel remote. He realises and takes my hand. I don't resist. All of a sudden I say that I want to make love, that I want him inside of me. Crude. He isn't surprised, or at least doesn't let it show. He comes close and strokes my face. We undress and he caresses me gently, kisses my breasts and sex. I spread my legs and wait for him to penetrate me. My libido's muted and I'm not aroused at all. When he senses that I'm dry, he applies lube and tries to enter me.

'Go on! All the way!'

I could have been a drill sergeant on the parade ground. He obeys, very carefully. I get no pleasure from the friction of that hard flesh inside of me, on the contrary. I can't bear the weight of a male. The same question forms in my head: I've gotten rid of my penis, so why would I want someone else's? The sensation is the same as last time, total rejection. But I let him continue, because I want to find out what it's like for a man to come in a woman's vagina. He takes longer, but then ejaculates. Like a toad spitting in my guts. I feel dirty. After a few seconds he withdraws and seems slightly dazed. What do I do with the semen inside me? Why this seed if I have no womb? I'm sterile, incapable of engendering life. Or only art, which is the creative fecundity of the infecund. I feel nauseous and make a dash for the bathroom. There's nothing to throw up, but I take a shower. I want to wash myself clean, with water, ever more water, washing away the filthy seed. I direct the shower head between my legs and think of a garden being watered from the sewer. Raül has shaken off his lethargy and comes in. Ever the loyal friend, he helps me to dry myself, but I feel detached from a presence I don't welcome. I've just reclaimed my body for myself, but I feel simultaneously guilty and happy. I thank Raül for everything. He confesses that he's never had sex like it, and praises my body and the depth of my vagina… I listen to him, all the while thinking that my revenge is complete. And then immediately I start tormenting myself for having put my love for my classmate to the test, risked the exhibition and our future together. I wonder how I'll be with her. Raül senses my anxiety and suggests we go out for dinner. I turn him down and say goodbye.

I walk down the street but feel like I'm running away from something. I speed up and almost collide with a man turning the corner.

'You're a bit keen, aren't you?' he says.

I look him up and down and spit in his face. I feel lighter, as though I've purged myself of Raül's dead semen.

Be well.
Ruth

PART THREE
(*Final Situation*)

Letter 33

My dear friend,
    When it came to it, the gallery owner changed very little of the layout we'd proposed. The exhibition opens tomorrow! The catalogue looks great: all three of us are in there, the gallery owner on her own, and the two of us in the studio with our works. The text says very little about us, and instead theorizes the collection as a whole, and draws out particular elements of interest. About my work, it suggests that both vertical and horizontal sculptures become volumes that transcend themselves and invite us to sample what we are able to capture of the invisible: the quintessence of language and the light of other reality, which can only be glimpsed through the artist who is willing to take a risk and challenge the monopoly of a reality established by those who determine what is and what is not 'real', that is, through the actual creator of a fiction which as such nevertheless becomes more real than reality itself. Make sense of that, my friend!
    It says of my girlfriend's work that we find ourselves before the hyperrealism of a fragmented anatomy that invites us to recreate the correlation that converges in the signifying value of the human condition: our body reduced into sections by a multitude of offers and referents that ultimately dismember us.
    The catalogues and invitations have been sent out to everybody of note. This exhibition marks the beginning of a new life that breaks completely with the past. It's a dream to see so many of our pieces arranged around the room. While my friend and the gallery owner talk in the office, I wander around, savouring my work. As I look, I have the sensation that nothing of this has come from my hands, my head, my desire. These twists, the sharpened steel and aluminium ridges, the bronze-hessian mesh, are these not to some degree my emancipation

and condemnation converted into aesthetic language and become a fount of knowledge? The knowledge that the artist alone belongs in freedom, or rather, beyond the non-social. My repressed possibilities, my deformed condition as a person, all of this is gone, and in its place is the operation to transgress the model by which they force us to be the same as the majority.

My girlfriend and the gallery owner emerge from the office in high spirits. The three of us hug and my friend suggests we have a drink back at hers. The gallery owner accepts, but I excuse myself saying that I'm tired. They go off in one direction, and I go in the other, hearing their laughter as they head uptown.

I walk quickly, again as though fleeing. It's dark. The street girls are hanging around, waiting for clients. I watch them and don't know whether I admire or detest them. I stop at a crossroads and one of the prostitutes comes up to me.

'This is my patch, get lost. If my pimp sees you, you're dead meat.'

I start walking, and then sense that I'm being followed. I turn around and see a good-looking, well-dressed man. He smiles at me.

'How about I take you to dinner,' he asks. 'What do you think?'

The other two will be having dinner without me, I think to myself, so I'll have dinner without them. And as I don't say no, the stranger takes my hand and we walk.

'I thought you might be about to get into some trouble there where you'd stopped. I know you didn't mean anything by it, but one of the girls might have decided you were taking their business. Each hooker has her own patch, as agreed between the pimps. These are situations and territory that no-one dares violate, and you didn't realise that stopping there for just a few seconds was enough for one of them to view you as an intruder. One only has to look at you for a moment to know that you're not one of them.'

I listen to his explanation, curious about a world that is unknown to me. We hail a taxi and he gives the driver an address. He sits close to me and rests his smooth hand on mine. He kisses me softly. The other two will probably be kissing. He pecks me on the cheek, and then on the lips. The taxi draws up by a restaurant. We're met by a uniformed doorman who opens the door and accompanies us inside. The head waiter approaches.

'Your usual table, sir?'

I feel awkward.

'Am I dressed smartly enough?' I whisper into my companion's ear.

He smiles. 'Everyone wears what they want these days.'

We crossed a lavish hall and a dining room divided into smaller, more intimate spaces and sit at a quiet table. I gaze at the napkins, the cutlery, the crystal glasses, and candelabra. The maitre d'hotel sets a match to the candles. Music, perhaps a nocturne, drifts across as though part of the light. He asks if my companion would like his usual order and, without asking me, my new friend nods and smiles. So far he has behaved like a gentleman who clearly likes the finer things. They serve us pink caviar and champagne.

'Let's drink a toast, to us,' he says, his voice trembling slightly. His eyes are shining as he looks at me, full of tenderness.

'To us!'

'To us.'

The champagne is excellent, and perfectly suited to the caviar which he shows me how to eat, on small crackers spread with butter.

'It's the first time I...'

We drink long, and he touches my hand reassuringly.

'I had to learn too; no-one is born knowing these things.'

I like his steady, velvety voice; and his eyes, which seem more transparent than the moisture that lives in them; and his soft, smooth hand on mine. We drink more champagne and kiss. The other two must be kissing, but with red wine and sandwiches. My heart is full of joy.

'I'm not sure I want to know, but why did you choose me to-night?'

'I didn't choose you. You appeared, and I saw you were in danger. You didn't belong on the street corner; then I liked you, straightaway... you have a certain class, you're different...'

What will the other two be saying to each other? I'm enjoying the words I hear. I'm dying to ask what he does for a living, how he affords his lifestyle, but it's not the right moment.

'Would you mind my asking what you do?' he asks.

'I'm a Fine Arts graduate.'

'And have you exhibited your work yet?'

'My first exhibition opens tomorrow.'

He asks me what the gallery's called.

'I know it. Do you have a workshop?'

'I use a friend's workshop. We were at university together, and we're exhibiting jointly.'

'So you don't have a workshop.'

'No.'

'You won't make a career in art without a workshop.'

We start a second bottle of champagne and they serve us salmon and avocado. What divine fish! Seeing my obvious enjoyment, he kisses me. When we've drunk half the bottle, he takes my hand again, squeezes it, kisses it, and says:

'I love you…'

'But…'

'I love you…'

The other two must be saying 'I love you' too.

'You can't possibly, you don't know me, we met each other less than an hour ago…'

'You have style, class, your walk is an elegant bodily calligraphy…'

I thought… I remember how quickly my sculptor friend and I got together. The champagne enables me to see the reality beyond it, as if all of a sudden it has transformed into a circumstance superior to itself, into an actuality that has never existed but is now present. I feel isolated and invaded by an extraordinary insight. The champagne allows me to understand reality as if cutting through time and even my desire-gripped consciousness. I feel powerful, proud. And we continue drinking.

When we've finished the salmon, we're served a small, very thick fillet of beef with crushed potato which we season with black pepper and a drizzle of olive oil. We drain the last of the champagne and are then presented with a French red; it's a vintage reserved for my companion. I taste the beef and wonder in astonished silence how such exquisite meat is possible. And the wine is perfect…

'I take pleasure in my friends' enjoyment of food…'

And he kisses me. They must kiss too, and drink, but cheap table wine. I realise I'm being cruel. He sees that something's amiss.

'A disagreeable thought just flashed through your mind… Resist anything that might upset you… Right now you're with me and you're happy…'

I gaze at him and now it's me who kisses him, hungrily, my tongue searching for his.

'Thank you, but there'll be time for that…'

This dinner turns my history upside-down, a history that so far I have carried within me like a rock. I don't really know what I'm saying, but whisper:

'I love you…'

We have ice cream for dessert, and coffee. Afterwards he asks if I'd like a whisky. I say yes, and we're brought two generous measures without ice or water. Two mouthfuls later I know I can become the most celebrated sculptor in the world. I say it aloud.

'I'll help you,' he replies.

When we leave the table I struggle to walk without drawing attention to myself, and I have to lean on his arm. The restaurant is paradise, immaterial matter, a sculpture whose interior has become brilliance that allows everything to be seen as though beyond itself.

A taxi is waiting outside and we get in, he with an easy elegance, and me however I can. He gives an address. It's a while before we arrive at a huge mansion in the hills above the city. He half-carries me to the gates, which open automatically via an electronic switch. A servant is standing there, and my companion dismisses him, saying that we're not to be disturbed.

We climb a sweeping marble staircase that opens onto a landing.

In spite of all the alcohol consumed, I'm aware of everything that's happening. We go into a large room with a high ceiling, furnished in the French style. I walk around as though I'm in a gallery or salesroom. I'm too warm, and start taking off my clothes. He watches me from an armchair and pours himself another whisky from a side table nearby. I ask where the bathroom is, and he gestures towards a door. I take a shower, and towelling myself, I walk back into the main room.

'I'll be back in a moment,' he says.

He goes towards the bathroom. As I'm in such a good mood, I pour a whisky and wander around the room. Suddenly a strange force stops me in front of the bathroom door. He is stood there, naked. I look at him, examine him. My eyes paint his entire physique. I shout out. It isn't possible, yet it is: he isn't he; he's her, a woman: breasts, sex, skin... My surprise becomes astonishment and then euphoria.

'I don't know who you are,' I say, going up to her, 'but I love you.'

Be well.
Ruth

My friend,

The opening was a huge success, and so many people turned up! And critics. The biggest surprise was that my family were there – mother, father, my sister, and also Raül. They tell me they saw the announcement in the paper. My sculptor girlfriend and I had really dressed to impress, to the extent that we almost became the party's main attraction.

Mother receives me with her claws out but I ignore everything she has to say, including the insults. She still refuses to accept any aspect of who I am, but I expect this, because it – I'm – really not easy to understand. She is wedded to her identity as the mother of a son, and is incapable of conceding anything that might threaten her desire.

'Don't you realise how ridiculous you look? This ludicrousness?'

Father, on the other hand, is approving. He congratulates me as an artist himself and shares in this success. My sister and Raül stick close by me, perhaps too close, because they occupy my attention and I'm not able to network as much as I want with the other guests. But I finally detach myself when I'm required to talk to the TV and press people. They ask me so many questions that I don't have answers for, but my girlfriend and the gallery owner help out. These men and women hang their reporting on a bunch of commonplaces that have nothing to do with how a work of art comes about. One of our Fine Arts professors had warned us about critics and journalists in case we should find ourselves exhibiting our work at some stage. One of the most frequent questions is: 'Why do this if no-one else is doing it?'

At about nine o'clock, someone I don't know appears and expresses an interest in my work.

'I'm only interested in your work, Ruth,' he says, bluntly.

The man is nothing special, by which I mean not especially attractive; he's stocky, slovenly dressed but seems to know exactly what he wants. Very carefully and deliberately, he examines each of my pieces in turn, taking in every angle. Once he has a good sense of the collection, he approaches the gallery owner and point blank declares:

'I want all of Ruth's work. How much?'

All three of us are taken aback, because we hadn't even considered putting a value on our work. The gallery owner is more used to the art business and shoots me a questioning glance. She politely asks the buyer to wait a moment and takes me into her office.

'What shall we ask for? What would seem like a good price?'

I don't speak, can't speak, because I have no idea, and my head can't deal with numbers.

'There's a lot of pieces. How about we say twenty million, ten for you and ten for me?'

My head's spinning. I'm not ready for this.

'Let's try, see what happens.'

We emerge from the office, the gallery owner makes her way over to the client, and with practised aplomb, communicates the asking price. Impassive, he asks if we can go into the office, where he sits down, takes out his chequebook and, without ceremony, makes out a cheque for twenty million.

'If you could let me have a receipt, please, and I also need to know when the exhibition closes.'

He makes to leave, and we accompany him to the door. The gallery owner is jubilant, hugging and kissing me. And then without delay she sets about sticking red dots on all my pieces to indicate that they're sold. When my father sees what's happening, he asks me if it's a joke or if one single person really has bought my whole collection. My friend and creator of the other half of the exhibition pieces gives me a tearful hug.

'What happened? Who was it?'

'Everything was so sudden, mysterious, I just don't understand. I can't explain it.'

The gallery owner says that she's never seen anything like it. 'Since we've sold half the exhibition so effortlessly, I'm going to give it my all now to try to get the other half placed.'

And she embraces my friend. The press are still in attendance, so the owner takes advantage and breaks the news to them. That's when the literary, art and television journalists start to pay more attention to my work.

Just as the gallery owner is about to uncork a few bottles of cava so that we can toast the sale, two cases of champagne arrive. One of the delivery men hands an envelope to me. I take out a white card that says: 'I love you…' The gallery owner and my friend are intrigued.

'What's happening? What's this, another mystery?'

'I don't have the faintest idea.'

I show them the card. This sudden sale has broken something deep inside me. I feel like I've done something profoundly wrong, maybe even betrayed my friend, without whom none of this would have been possible. The workshop, materials, advice… I hold her close and kiss her sincerely, but there's an emotional distance now that will push us further apart.

At eleven o'clock we abandon the gallery, the three of us together. We make our way to her studio where we'd agreed to have a bite to eat. We drink, and barely eat anything. From time to time the painful silence is broken by a word or two. I feel awkward and decide to leave. We embrace again, through tears. I've gone less than a hundred metres or so when a car draws alongside. A hand appears from the rear window holding a fat envelope.

'It's for your studio-workshop.'

And the car drives off.

Take care.

Ruth

Letter 35

My dear friend,

As you can imagine, I couldn't wait to see my new workshop. It's a big space with all manner of work tools and instruments, and there's a small side room which could be used as an office, bedroom, even a dining kitchen, with fridge, sofa, table and chairs. On one of the walls of the workshop there's a large mirror. There's fantastic natural light and the electric lights are good too. I can't help but feel lonely. It's the grief of being away from my friend and establishing myself here means I have no choice but to leave her behind. A voice jolts me from my introspection.

'Are you comfortable here?'

I turn around and see my Francophile acquaintance. I'm surprised and speechless.

'I said I'd help you. I'm going to exhibit your work internationally, and I'll buy whatever's necessary until you become the most sought-after sculptor in the world. You're already on your way. From now on I'll be your dealer…'

I'm stunned. Everything that's happening to me is excessive, unreal, the stuff of dreams. But I feel good.

'You have talent, taste, and you're stunningly beautiful.'

He comes close and kisses me.

'I love you. I fell in love with you when I first saw you, and I've fallen in love with your work.' The voice resonates within me, as though it's generated there. He holds me and kisses me again. 'I never make mistakes where my feelings are concerned, or my judgements; I know too many people…'

He strokes me and starts to take off my clothes. When I'm naked, he asks me to undress him. I scream silently as though it's the first time I've seen him: he's a woman! He takes my arm and leads me to the big mirror. We gaze at our reflections. My eyes are wide with disbelief at what I'm seeing.

'We're both men!' I yell out in confusion.

In the mirror our female sexes have become male. I have my old penis back. And him? He reads my mind: 'Me too.'

I turn away from the mirror and look at him directly. I don't understand: we both have female sexes. I look in the mirror again: are sexes are male. He puts an arm around my shoulders.

'Which do you think is our true sex,' he asks, 'the real image or the virtual image in the mirror?' He pauses before saying, 'Who are you and I? Because what we want to be has nothing to do with what we can't help but be. We've ceased to be incomplete men, but are we fully women? It pleases me to dress as a man because I know that there will always be something male about me. You look so elegant dressed as a woman. We make an exquisite couple.'

He kisses me. His words don't seem at all strange to me. We put on our clothes and look at ourselves again in the mirror. He's right, we look good together. We smile. He guides me over to the side room and takes a bottle of champagne from the fridge. He pours two glasses and we drink a toast to our identities. As we sit on the sofa he talks and I contemplate. Two different discourses with the same point of origin that diverge as they unfold.

'Work, work hard… We'll see each other again in a year's time.'

My friend, what's happening to me? Imaginings, dreams, fantasies, illusions, all more powerful than brittle reality. Perhaps everything is exaggerated precisely to demonstrate that it's real. I despise this studio. I want to work with my girlfriend.

That evening I drop by the gallery for an update. There's no-one there except the owner. The room is an immense desert, and the pieces on display seem to have no meaning. Oh! I realise suddenly that all the red dots have disappeared from my sculptures. The expression on my face surprises the owner, who confesses that so far not a single work has been sold.

Be well.
Ruth

My friend,

I can scarcely contain my excitement when I decide to start work in my studio… an excitement I've given in to, having weighed things up and finally accepted that I am me and my sculptures. Ready to work. I'm realising my desire at last. In this workshop I will create my masterpiece. My workshop, mine… But I have to tell you something really disconcerting: even though I knew where it was, I can't locate it. What's happened to it? Convinced that I must be lost, I go back home to look for the address amongst the papers that my Francophile acquaintance gave me. I can't find the envelope, and there's no trace of the documentation. I try to remember and return to the spot where I first visited the workshop, but I don't recognize the place. I wander around the neighbourhood, utterly bewildered. Nothing. The houses are familiar, the offices, shops, warehouses, church, doorways… But there's no sign of my studio-workshop. It was there! I spent time inside it and I can describe the layout to you from memory. I do another few circuits of the neighbourhood and then give up. Leaning back against a wall, my mind is a blank. The reality I've experienced can't simply disappear; it's an objective reality perceived intensely. Or maybe it never existed? I head instinctively for the gallery. I mention the red dots and the cheque for twenty million to the owner. She looks bemused and asks if I'm feeling alright.

I'm picking up this letter again after speaking with the psychoanalyst. I was expecting him to spout a load of nonsense at me. He says that I've been suffering hallucinations. As if! I know very well what I've experienced: what I've seen, felt, and touched. His advice is that I need immediate treatment. Adopting a protective tone, he explains that my perceptions lack external objects, that I'm living a falsification of reality fed by entities beyond the grasp of my consciousness, and that without being aware of it, I'm transgressing the rule of my normal behaviour… What gibberish! But he expands further: apparently I'm protagonizing a reality that isn't real, a reality that's the offspring of my desire. I tell him he's talking rubbish, that these are facile interpretations, manias of his profession designed to complicate my life. No-one can deny the reality of what I've seen, felt, and touched. No-one. To admit that this is all false would be tantamount to admitting that I'm mad, that I've lost my senses. And I've never felt more sound-minded. I walk out.

Back home I concede that some of the things I've experienced recently are certainly odd. Beginning to get worried, I go to see my sculptor girlfriend, impelled by the force of necessity. I tell her everything, from the day I met my mysterious benefactor until now. She listens intently and seems frequently amazed at what I say. Because it was an experience we shared, I talk in detail about the gallery opening. She is adamant.

'Neither you nor I sold any of our work, and we served cava, not champagne.'

With emotion in her voice, my friend confides that during and after the opening, she thought my behaviour was quite bizarre, as if I were somehow absent and not my usual self. I suggest that we undress. When we're naked we move to her bedroom where there's a large mirror, and I position us so that we're both in the frame. I study our reflections closely and choke: she has a woman's sex, of course, but mine is male, I have a penis just like the one that tortured me for so many years. In spite of my shock, or perhaps because of it, I ask:

'What do you see?'

'You, beautiful as always.'

'And I'm not different, changed in any way?' I gesture towards my groin.

'Your sex is very pretty.'

With this information in mind, I look at my body directly and I can see that I have a female sex. Even so, I can't resist taking another look in the mirror. My friend has left the room and I'm alone. I go right up to the mirror. I observe myself with focussed concentration: yes, it's a penis. Seeing it isn't enough, and I touch myself. I can feel a vulva, but in the mirror my hand is on a penis. Reeling and not thinking, I run to find my friend and launch myself at her, shouting,

'I want to penetrate you, I'm a man and you want me to play being a woman. I'm a man, a man…!'

I burst into floods of tears and lose all sense of anything. When I come to, I'm on a stretcher. My friend is at my side.

'Where am I? What happened?'

'We're going to hospital because you're not well…'

They keep me in for three or four days and when I come out, I'm utterly drained.

I'll let you know how I am.

Take care.
Ruth

My dearest friend,

The hospital discharged me to my parents' home. The first day they were like strangers. I kept asking myself: 'What do these people want?' And because from time to time I get agitated, they give me sedatives. I want to leave. A tongue in flames or feet that walk on burning embers. I cannot abide mother. The closer she is to me, the more monstrous she appears. Blood that drowns my pillowcase from the cadaverous arms wanting to seize me. Unblinking monster that scrutinizes the sex she says I have and don't have. Most of the time I'm feverish. I'm losing a lot of weight. Father doesn't seem to be here, but I can sense his calm. I want to return to the trees where the sparrows roost and incubate the virginity of horizons. I want to go back to my studio, claim the ten million I'm owed from the sale of my work. I don't trust the gallery owner, she's too chic and too fond of expensive cars. For example, the other day I saw her from the balcony driving a Rolls. Even though it was a way off, I could make out the model and even the number plate. From the fifth floor, which counting the main floor and the mezzanine, is the seventh. No height is enough, I'm a renowned sculptor who's sold everything at her first exhibition. Do you know what mother said to me the other day? That she keeps the penis from when I was born in the drawer of her bedside table. Once when I was asleep she placed it between my legs, on my pubis, and stood looking at it for ages, and then she took a Polaroid. Every now and again she screams:

'I had a son! Now I've got him back. He's my son. Extinguish the sea and raze the mountain. Don't let them take him! He's mine! No eyes dare look at him: he's mine! Silences crown him with live flesh: he's mine!'

I'm writing to you in secret because they spy on me. One day mother came across a letter that I wrote to you years ago but couldn't send because the post offices had run out of carrier pigeons. Now I'm using my sister; she makes a great falcon. I spend a lot of time on the balcony, drawn by the hospital moons in mourning and pallid setts. I realise how insignificant the concierge is. The gallery owner is dead. My girlfriend has fled before the mortally wounded stones. My eyes weigh heavy and my heartbeat is so weak it is scarcely audible. My whole body drags me downwards as though it is moved by earth's centripetal force. I am on the balcony. Everyone tramples on the nakedness of History: drunken blind brightness, infinite night of starched shrouds. I am on the balcony and now and then I skip along the rail. Behind me, infinite copies of my penis spurt from the banister of desire. Who has swept away my woman's sex? I know: there is nothing more dirty than the sea's anxiety. I am on the balcony. The candelabra of bones renounce the lips while vaginas catch the metropolitan marches of orphanhood. Call me, my friend; catch the image that's about to dissolve in the orphanhood of surrender. Once the streetlights have gone out, falling from the balcony I'll extinguish myself in the ashes of all cemeteries… desert of myself, eviction never inhabited, impossible nest, useless fermentation… While first light adorns restfulness, time will keep the memory of no-one.

I hope you will be happy. Goodbye.
Ruth